DOORS

Other Fiction by William Hoffman

Novels
    The Trumpet Unblown
    Days in the Yellow Leaf
    A Place for My Head
    The Dark Mountains
    Yancey's War
    A Walk to the River
    A Death of Dreams
    The Land That Drank the Rain
    Godfires
    Furors Die
    Tidewater Blood

Short-Story Collections
    Virginia Reels
    By Land, by Sea
    Follow Me Home

DOORS

Stories by William Hoffman

University of Missouri Press
Columbia and London

Library of Congress Cataloging-in-Publication Data

Hoffman, William, 1925–
    Doors : stories / by William Hoffman.
       p.   cm.
    ISBN 0-8262-1238-7 (alk. paper)
    1. United States—Social life and customs—20th century—Fiction.
I. Title
PS3558.034638D66   1999
813'.54—dc21   98-56143
                                                                  CIP

♾ ™ This paper meets the requirements of the
American National Standard for Permanence of Paper
for Printed Library Materials, Z39.48, 1984.

Text designer: Stephanie Foley
Cover design: Mindy Shouse
Typesetter: Crane Composition, Inc.
Printer and binder: Edwards Brothers, Inc.
Typefaces: Adobe Garamond, Caligraphy, and Emancipation

"Doors," "Stones," and "Place" were published in *Shenandoah*. "Stones" was also published in the *O'Henry Prize Stories, 1996*. "Roll Call" and "Blood" were published in the *Virginia Quarterly Review*. "Landings," "Winter Wheat," "Prodigal," "Humility," and "Tenant" were published in *The Sewanee Review*.

For Dabney Stuart

CONTENTS

DOORS   1

PRODIGAL   19

PLACE   39

ROLL CALL   57

HUMILITY   75

STONES   96

BLOOD   115

LANDINGS   134

TENANT   155

WINTER WHEAT   174

DOORS

DOORS

He was presumptuous and loose-mouthed, not that I didn't like talking myself but believed it unseemly in a man, especially Horace Puckett. Horace Horsecollar I called him, that first name a mockery of the Latin poet, one of whose Sabine odes I'd translated during my senior year at St. Elizabeth's by the Sea.

Horace Horsecollar arrived to fix my furnace. I'd been left the house by my father, who for seventeen years and to the day he died served as chairman of the Board of Supervisors for Howell County, Virginia, a tobacco-growing region shaped like a teardrop dangling above central North Carolina. You couldn't throw a stone to the border, but you might've reached it with birdshot.

I was no prude. I'd been married to a slim, lovely man who made good money selling cemeteries through the pine-ragged region. Some would not consider that a lofty business, but the South reverences graveyards.

He'd drive to a small community, find fifty acres in an outlying district—often sprouting pigweed, honeysuckle, thistles—and purchase the land to clear and seed it with fescue, pampas grass, and weeping willows. He'd next asphalt access roads. At the center he'd build a knoll on which to erect a concrete statue of Christ holding two sleeping lambs.

1

"Thumb rule is thirty people got to be planted before I come out whole on the deal," Henry had calculated, meaning that number needed to meet their Maker.

Course his own plot cost him nothing. As he sat at the table eating eggs over, link sausage, and grits, he looked at me as if about to ask a question. Words never emerged from his lips. He bowed to his plate in a close-eyed silent devotion.

I laid him out on the breakfast-room floor and called Dr. Belotte, though I saw by the distant set in Henry's china blue eyes the phone was no use. Country folk learn early the sight of death, which is as common as ticks, Jap beetles, and corn-house mice.

My Henry left me well fixed. I kept the business running till a man from Danville named MacMasters bought it. I then drove to the Planter's National Bank and got Carrington Epes, the president, to invest the money in stocks and bonds. Each quarter Carrington stopped by my house carrying a report. I saved more than I spent, which my father taught me, saying, "What you don't need, you won't miss; and what you won't miss, you don't need."

When my father died, I inherited his money and that house too, which had belonged in the family five generations. My Henry and I'd never had children, and sometimes I felt lonely. Men asked me out to dine, but I figured they were primarily chasing my dollars. People said I was too particular.

The house been built a piece at a time, a bedroom added here, a parlor there, as needed. Bricks baked of clay right on the place had been pocked by Yankee bullets, and horseshoe prints scarred the front stairs where a Connecticut captain had galloped his horse to the second floor to saber down a chandelier. Often the rooms were cold even during June.

I toured England, France, and Italy. Several times a year I drove my Buick to Raleigh or Winston-Salem to see a play and attend the opera. Mostly I enjoyed staying home keeping up my garden and collecting antique silver napkin rings. I owned one authenticated to have belonged to Dolly Madison.

The furnace gave trouble. It was old, ugly, a beast installed when every room had been used, an oil burner that circulated hot water. I phoned a Farmville heating contractor, who sent out a uniformed repairman driving a shiny red van that had on the side a coat of arms that resembled a golden commode seat surrounding two plumber's helpers rampant. He scratched his head, fingered a pocket calculator, and gave me a price for replacement that took my breath.

I gave to charity, never to foolishness. I solicited and received other bids, higher and lower, all outrageous. "They don't make them anymore," was a refrain that beat my ears. While I was having my hair done at the Little Ritz Hair Salon, Windy Belle, the ageless flame-headed proprietress, suggested Horace Puckett.

"He's good fixing," Windy said. "Saved the pump at the middle school. Would've cost county money set aside to paint the water tank."

I phoned the Dew Drop Inn where Horace reportedly checked by daily. He didn't own a line himself. I found that unpromising. Still I left word, and he appeared at the house on a damp, blowing Wednesday when my maid, Lucinda, took her half day off. He drove a poky black Ford truck that must've been around when pickups were first hatched. It did appear clean and well maintained.

I expected a big man, but he was short, chunky, and you could've bounced a ball through those bowlegs. He had a bushy black mustache. He wore sagging gray coveralls, a leather jacket, and a billed blue cap that displayed a green largemouth bass leaping after a golden dragonfly.

He knocked at my front door. I realized I'd seen him around Tobaccoton, possibly standing under shade of the courthouse elm during fierce heat of our southside summers or maybe in front of the Dark Leaf Warehouse during market days when the auctioneer's chant made dollar music for the planters.

"Heard you having trouble firing up," he said, his voice deliberate and not to be hurried. His accent was southern, but not Howell County southern.

I sent him around back to the outside basement entrance because I wasn't in the habit of letting laborers come through the front door or the kitchen one either if it could be avoided. I assumed he didn't know better. I switched on the basement lights and raised my palm to indicate the furnace. He set on steel-rimmed glasses, whistled, tipped back his cap, grinned. His oversized teeth protruded, his top lip never quite covering them.

"A furnace is the heart of a house," he said. "Ain't she a beauty?"

"Some have called this one a monster," I said.

"They don't know. She's a Minnesota Maid. Built in Duluth and originally burned coal. One thing you got to say about Yankees is they can put together a gauldern furnace. She sick huh?"

"She provides only feeble heat," I said, thinking how absurd it was to be using gender when talking about a machine.

"She's poorly then. Working good, she'd have you opening windows and switching on fans. I'll get a tool or two and have a peek I will."

"I trust you know what you're doing."

"Won't cost you a cent to find out," he said and gazed at me out of eyes the color of chestnuts, a direct and penetrating scrutiny, causing me to lean back as if nudged.

With a rolling gait he left the basement and returned to his pickup. The heavy toolbox he carried back made him list to his right. Large steel wrenches he lifted from it looked as if they'd been not only wiped but polished.

When he started tugging, pounding, and grunting, I left. Inside the house, his work banged through the pipes and radiators. I phoned Carrington Epes.

"Never heard a complaint about his work," Carrington said. "Had a note here at the bank and paid it off on time. Pretty much sticks to himself. Owns his house."

"He's making infernal noises in my basement."

"Don't suppose you can work on a furnace quietly," Carrington said, and I realized he was being patient with a fussy widow woman. I hung up.

I sat in the kitchen where I kept the electric cook stove switched on to stay warm. I also wore my hat, wool coat, and gloves. More hammering and screeching of rusty fixtures. When I could endure the noise no longer, I walked down the inside steps. Parts lay all over the concrete floor.

"Mineral deposits," Horace said. "Water around here. Mostly limestone calcium. Clogged your pipes."

"I do not have pipes," I said.

"This old gal does. You shivering upstairs?"

"I can survive as long as I'm confident you'll have her—it—fixed by dark. It's a cold house at the best of times."

"Doing my derndest," he said and winked. "Course my stomach's rubbing my backbone."

I fixed a ham sandwich and a bowl of bean soup, which I carried down to him. I didn't wait but left him eating standing up. When I again heard pipes clattering, I opened the basement door. He'd set his plate and bowl on the threshold.

At dark he was still working. I called my cousin Florence in Blackstone and asked could I come stay the night. Just as I finished packing a bag, all racket stopped, and the furnace hummed. I laid my hand on a radiator and felt heat seep into the iron conduits.

I went to the basement. Horace had gathered his tools and was sweeping. The furnace rumbled quietly. I looked at the water-pressure gauge as my Henry used to do. It read 20 psi, exactly what it was supposed to.

"She'll last if you care for her," Horace said. "Ought to have her gone over yearly. Clean her tubes."

"I'd like to contract with you to do that for me."

"Nope," he said, dumped his sweepings in the trash barrel, and put on his jacket and cap. "I work for people who think I'm good enough to be invited inside. You wouldn't even have me up to eat my soup and sandwich. I'm making out your bill here, which comes to forty dollars. It'd been less if you hadn't made me feel I smelled like a wet dog."

"I didn't mean to make you feel anything. I am a woman living alone."

"I know what you are and who I am," he said. He pinched a pencil stub from behind an ear and wrote on a pad pulled from a jacket pocket. He presented the bill. He had a nice hand, the printing precise and level across the page. "I wouldn't've come in your house. I just expected to be treated respectful."

"I'm sorry," I said. "I don't like hurting anyone's feelings."

"I have yet to mark your bill paid," he said. "No credit."

I gave him my check, stood at a parlor window, and watched him drive off. What bothered me more than his ridiculous feelings was the likelihood I'd need him again during the winter to tend the brute.

He'd displayed a certain countrified dignity and obviously possessed a talent with machinery, which he thought of as female, but I wasn't really sorry I'd not allowed him in my house. After all on leaving, he'd smelled strongly of tobacco, fuel oil, and sweat.

I didn't see Horace Horsecollar again till summer, a July scorcher, the roadside dust swirling and abrasive, the birds too heat-smitten to move off the tree limbs or the power lines. I'd driven to downtown Tobaccoton for my dental appointment, and as I was leaving Dr. Moss's office over the Acme Drugstore a man at the curb called out, "Long live the queen."

Horace didn't just remove his cap. As he bowed he swept it almost to the gritty sidewalk. The gesture unbalanced him, and he staggered drunk. He began attempting to unbutton his coveralls. A pale, stooped man wearing paint-spattered Levi's and a sleeveless T-shirt walked from the drugstore and righted him.

"Got no coat," Horace said. "Need to spread something on the ground so Queenie don't dirty her shoes."

"Sorry, lady," the man said. He supported Horace and

moved him away along the sidewalk. People watched and whispered.

"Disgusting," I said to Carl Pickney, the town policeman. "You're not going to arrest him?"

"Hate to do that," Carl said, his face ruddy, his meaty thumbs hooked over the thick black leather belt of his gray uniform. "Had a daughter who died."

I felt shame, though at the moment there was nothing I could do. The pale stooped man helped Horace on down the street. Horace still attempted to unbutton his coveralls. I drove home, stewed, and called Ike St. Clair. Ike was Tobaccoton's mayor and the John Deere tractor dealer. He knew everything about everybody in town and around Howell County.

"Car wreck," he said. "A year ago while you were in Europe. Killed the girl. Pretty little sixteen-year-old, her Honda rammed by a logging truck. Horace awarded a court judgment, but the truck owner carried no insurance. Horace had big bills to meet at the Farmville hospital."

"Not natives of the county," I said. "Otherwise I'd have heard."

"From the Tennessee hills. Not much formal education but a proud man. Wife already dead. Stayed around to work and pay the bills. Got into Howell County helping install the heating plant at the high school. Been here since. Went on a fling remembering the girl's birthday. Those mountain folks keep to their own code."

"He's talented with furnaces," I said.

"Word is he can fix everything but a broken heart," Ike said.

So I naturally felt terrible, yet didn't know how to show

contrition. I couldn't send flowers to a man. I sat at my rosewood Queen Anne secretary and wrote him a note, explaining I'd just heard of his misfortune and wanted to express my sympathy. I asked whether he had a favorite charity I might contribute to.

I received no acknowledgement. Perhaps I shouldn't have expected any. Men didn't answer notes, at least his kind wouldn't. At September's first chill, I nervously switched on the creature, but it, she, worked perfectly. I felt benign vibrations through my heart-of-pine floors, and the crystal quivered faintly in my china cabinet.

The ferociously cruel winter didn't strike till mid-January, and then it seemed the wind intended to scythe Howell County off the face of the earth. Ice storms followed by swirling snows battered us. Everywhere branches broke from trees, fracturing a thousand limbs.

Electric lines snapped. The fiend couldn't run without power, and despite Lucinda and I toting wood to fireplaces till we became frazzled, radiators in the upstairs bedrooms froze. When heat did clank back on, they burst, and my house became flooded with cascades of water. Then arctic cold assaulted us a second time, and icicles hung from the parlor ceiling.

For the remainder of the winter, I moved in with cousin Florence. She owned a modern brick house—small, tight, confining. I was accustomed to space and lived in a frenzy of worry about my possessions. I had brought along my silver napkin rings, jewelry, and a photograph of Henry. The grim winter seemed endless, fraught with sleet, freezing rain, and evil winds till April. There were days I believed the sun and warmth would never again bless this earth.

When I returned to Tobaccoton, I could find no one to fix my house. Our entire populace suffered repair problems. Carpenters, electricians, and plumbers were all spoken for. The few who came just to take a look at my trouble shook their heads. Too big a job, they said. The old houses were difficult to deal with at the best of times.

I thought of Horace. "Fix everything but a broken heart." I remembered you reached him at the Dew Drop Inn. I called and left my number.

I heard nothing. I was now staying at the Farmville Motel, my lodging paid for through homeowner's coverage. I again phoned Ike at the mayor's office. He gave me Horace's address.

I drove north of town, crossed Rosemary Creek, and found the house at the end of a dirt road—tiny, white clapboard, yet neat, freshly painted, storm windows, no mess, the yard growing grass that had been mowed and raked. A tire swing hung by a rope from the limb of a hackberry. Nobody answered my knock. To his door I pinned a note pleading desperation. I underlined the word *Please.*

Horace surprised me Saturday afternoon. I didn't hear him drive up in the same ancient pickup. Lucinda was washing windows and I working in my garden planting a row of snap beans. We'd been keeping house the best we could, but it had taken on an abandoned, forlorn appearance. Nothing seemed in order.

Once the garden had been my refuge, but now the soil betrayed me and felt hard, unyielding, the enemy. I pounded my hoe against hateful jagged clods. The blows jarred my arms, causing a shoulder to ache so badly I couldn't sleep on that side.

"Clay," Horace said behind me. "You ought to cover her with cow droppings and lime, plow her under, let her rest a year, and then plow her again."

"You're kind to come," I said, thinking gardens like machinery possessed female gender. "I'm very sorry about the losses in your family."

"Well I reckon I'm sorry about the way I behaved downtown," he said. "Don't usually act the fool. Likely you're wanting me to fix up your house."

"I'd be obliged if you'd look and tell me what you're able to do."

"I expect this is one time you'll have to let me through the door," he said.

I thought it best to let the remark pass. He entered with me from the back porch. He put on his glasses and stayed less than five minutes strolling through rooms, his hands clasped behind him. When he left by way of the kitchen, I waited for him to spit as most men do before making decisions, even some well-bred ones. Horace didn't.

"Can and will do the work," he said.

"About the price," I said, noticing his coveralls were creased and his mustache had been trimmed. He undoubtedly believed in order.

"Won't charge you more than anyone else," he said.

I hesitated. I wanted numbers written down. Still I remembered his reputation for honest work, and I was so desperate I would've agreed to most anything except selling my napkin rings.

"That's satisfactory," I said. "I'll pay your bill."

He reset his cap, walked to his pickup, and backed it to the house. Using those long-handled wrenches that were so immaculate he began freeing the burst radiators. Because they were extremely heavy, he drove into town and returned with a black man named Ben Randolph to help carry the radiators out. When Horace quit that night, he hauled them off.

He went at the house full tilt, arriving mornings just at daybreak, working till noon, and taking twenty minutes for lunch. He ate sandwiches he carried in a paper sack and drank coffee from his thermos while sitting under shade of the pecan tree in the back yard. He obviously didn't expect me to feed him.

When town water was cut on and Lucinda and I were able to use my kitchen, I offered him a chicken leg and slice of my brown sugar pie. I made a point of inviting him to come through the kitchen door, and he accepted. I seated him not in the kitchen but at the breakfast-room table. He removed his cap and with bowed head gave a silent, lip-moving thanks. It was pleasant once again to feed a man.

"He work a mule into the grave," Lucinda said. A white cloth tied about her head, she moved slowly but steadily. Her children clipped my hedges, raked my leaves, and gathered blackberries that grew around the pond in the low ground.

Horace did seem to know how to do everything. He tore down plaster, replaced wiring, and installed new lathing. I occasionally stopped my work to watch him. He had short, stubby fingers, yet as they soldered copper joints or mitered strips of molding, they appeared artistic too, so surely placed and seeming to possess instinct and knowledge without specific direction from him.

While I watched him thread and precisely fit a pipe into a T-coupling, those hands caused me to undergo a sensual experience, a feeling very much as if his fingers had touched my bare breasts. Quickly I turned away. The incident was ridiculous and embarrassing. I never told anybody, not even my cousin Florence or my closest friend Emily Baskerville.

I offered to pay Horace the Saturday afternoon of each week. He did turn over to me the invoices from Birdsong Brothers Building & Supply but never asked for wages.

"Just as soon hold off till I complete the job," he said, using his limp cap to wipe sweat from his porous forehead. The summer continued hot and dry, the air woolly, flaying, the dust never settling. Often Horace seemed at the center of that dust.

"You must need money," I said, a bit uneasy. I liked to know exactly where I stood with any undertaking. Still I was very pleased with his work.

"No'm, I don't. Maybe I look poorboy, but they glad to see me down at the bank. Besides you might not be altogether satisfied with the work I'm doing around your place."

"I can tell you right here and now such won't be the case," I said and smiled. He simply stared, those unblinking chestnut eyes again making me feel I'd been nudged.

I was picking up my life in the community. I played cards twice a week and took part in the St. Matthew's Summer Bazaar where I sold cakes, pies, and favors. I gave a bridal party for the daughter of Elvira Lilly, another dear friend. Truth is many people looked to me socially because both my father and my Henry had been so prominent in Tobaccoton. I was certainly the best bridge player and the only lady who'd ever been to an inaugural ball at the governor's mansion.

By summer's end, Horace had nearly completed his work. I was again able to live in my house. He still had to refinish floors and weld the old dragon's boiler, which had split a seam. When all was done, I intended to give a party.

Finally, the second week in September, a chilly rainy day, he turned on heat. I sat upstairs in my bedroom but sensed a slight tremor through the house. I crossed to a front window and laid my fingers on the radiator. Within minutes I felt warmth.

I hurried down the steps to the back porch. He was carrying tools from the basement to his truck. He looked dirty, weary, the cold drizzle streaking black smudges down his face. I smiled at his bowlegged gait, careful not to let him see.

" 'Bout done all I can 'round here," he said.

"Come in the kitchen while I get my checkbook," I said. I'd really grown rather fond of him. Nobody could've been more devoted to a job. I again had my house well and whole.

"Don't need your checkbook," he said and wiped rain from his face as he stood at the foot of the steps. He peered up at me, his wet mustache drooping.

"You'll catch your death out here," I said. "Are you telling me you need time to tote up your bill?"

"Nope I don't."

"What then?" I asked and felt a twinge of alarm. I wished he weren't standing in the mean drizzle.

"You sure you pleased with your house?"

"Indeed I am. I've bragged on you to all the ladies. Do you need pencil and paper? I have them in the kitchen."

"No'm, though I may need a new shirt."

"You tore your shirt?" I asked, puzzled because he wore

only coveralls, each pair clean and pressed at the days'
beginnings.

"No'm. What I'd like is to accompany you to church
next Sunday. Regular service. Hope for you to take my arm
going up and down the steps. I want to sit beside you and
share a hymnbook. Afterwards be nice for you to introduce
me around so I can shake a few hands."

"I don't see how you can expect me to agree to that," I
said when I had control of my voice. I thought of Emily
Baskerville, Elvira Lilly, Mary Louise Vassour, and Bernice
Boatwright. I saw them seeing me enter St. Matthew's on
the arm of Horace Puckett. The very idea was too ridiculous for words.

"That's my price," he said, dripping. "You told me you'd
pay it. I took your word."

"I want to give you money," I said. "Any court in the
world would say all I owe is money."

"Won't be a court. Either you pay or you don't. You're
old enough to have learned money don't buy everything."

He turned and carried the last of his tools to his truck. I
entered the house both shocked and suppressing laughter.
His bill was so absurd as to be idiotic. I stopped. There I
stood in my warm and mended house. I thought of his fingers' grace and the beauty they'd restored. But to take him
to St. Matthew's when if he belonged to any denomination
at all it had to be to some evangelical, wailing sect of red-
necks. A new shirt. I would simply send him a check.

I sat at my secretary, calculated the number of weeks
he'd worked, and phoned the bank to ask Carrington Epes
the going hourly rate for carpenters. I then multiplied,
licked an envelope, and dropped the check in the mail.

It wasn't cashed. Each month when my bank statement

arrived I frowned at the entries. I didn't know what to do next. I thought of writing a second check. There was no more reason to believe he would cash it than the first. I phoned the Dew Drop Inn and left word for Horace to call. He did not.

Howell County suffered through another dreadful winter. The snowfall and early freeze set records, yet the furnace purred like a contented tiger—or tigress. Only when the electricity shut off for a few hours did I feel fright. I was able to entertain my bridge club and have Father Buford, our pastor at St. Matthew's, to dinner. Mornings as I drank hot tea, I watched icicles beneath the house's eaves lengthen and glitter. They became rainbow spectra in the sunlight.

With the flowering of dogwood blooms and the four-note plaints of mourning doves, a bad conscience continued to nag me. Horace had still not banked my check. I considered leaving cash on his doorstep, but that was foolish, the amount much too large, and anybody could pick it up. I thought perhaps he'd fled town, yet Saturday on my way to the Little Ritz I passed him in his truck. Though I raised my hand, he didn't appear to see me.

I spoke to Father Buford after Easter services. He was a slender young man who wore tweedy jackets with his clerical collars. Though only a few years out of the seminary and modern in many ways, I liked him but didn't care for his face squinching up in laughter when I mentioned my dilemma.

"You shrink from bringing a sheep into God's flock?" he asked. "You think we should allow only Howell County's finest to sit in our pews? Please, Flora, whom did Our Savior come to serve?"

I left the church ladened with guilt, drove across the

rain-swollen Rosemary Creek, and stopped before Horace's house. He sat on his little porch smoking a cigarette and reading the *Farmville Herald*. He wore a clean undershirt and khaki trousers but was barefooted. I'd scarcely ever seen my Henry's long, bony feet. Horace stood for me.

"If you'll call for me next Sunday at ten forty-five, I'll be ready," I said. "Are we to go in your pickup?"

"She don't buck," he said, no change of expression.

I lived the rest of the week in dread. I started to call the ladies, yet how to explain? I imagined their carryings-on behind my back. Phone lines would sizzle. I'd simply have to hold my head high and endure.

Horace arrived on time. Rather than let him come through the front door, I met him on the porch. He wore a dark stiff suit, a vest, a white shirt, and a brown tie. He doffed a gray fedora. His shoes were boxy and thickly soled. I suspected all his clothes were new.

"We might take my car," I offered.

"Nope," he said.

I could've worn a white dress. The interior of the pickup gleamed. He must've scoured every inch of it—or her. As we climbed the steps to the church, I obediently took his arm. I felt his firm strength. I intercepted amused glances from members of the congregation and held my eyes steady. Father Buford preached on "The Least of These." He grinned when he laid the host upon my tongue.

Afterwards I introduced Horace to those who stopped by my pew. Many men apparently knew him and seemed genuinely glad to have him at St. Matthew's. A few ladies simpered, but Emily and Elvira squeezed my hand.

Horace drove me home and accompanied me up to the front porch. The phone was ringing. I wondered which of the ladies would be first to call. Horace hesitated, no doubt waiting to be invited in.

I smiled, told him I expected him to cash my check, and turned to the door. He set his hat on squarely and without a word marched down the steps. As he walked toward his pickup, I saw that rigid pride and hurt dignity in his stride. He'd been a gentleman after his fashion. He was surely no horsecollar. I again remembered his hands, those fingers so full of assurance, tenderness, and repair.

I called to him. Lucinda's buttermilk biscuits and fried chicken were in the refrigerator. He returned toward the house, and when he climbed the steps, I started to direct him to wipe his feet on the mat but caught myself and merely opened the front door wide enough for us both to enter.

PRODIGAL

The commercial street leads southwestward from hazily sunlit Richmond, past strip malls, auto stores, garages, and cut-rate motels before broadening into suburban developments that have classy names like Foxcroft Acres, Beechwood, and Hunter's Trace.

I drive my van past a flowered gateway and a residential lake where Canadian honkers glide in stately procession across an olive surface and leave a wake. Beyond the gates are tidy, landscaped houses set on quarter-acre lawns shaded by maples, oaks, and Bradford pears.

If you drive far enough under the spring canopies of interlaced limbs, you'll reach tennis courts, the green expanse of golf courses, and white clubhouses, which are themselves temples of a sort.

Just as suddenly I am beyond the reach of city money, out into a countryside patched with small farms and an occasional fresh vegetable stand or white-planked store—this not Tidewater but red-clay country, a depressed part of Virginia clinging to land, not industry, to soybeans, dairies, the billet woods, and languidly growing tobacco.

Turn off the highway onto a narrow county road, as my penciled directions indicate, drive half a mile among broomstraw fields and slash pine woods, top a rise, and you come upon the Temple of Zion, not a little hick church, but a Jeffersonian structure of major proportions, classic, columned, porticoed, the mortar gleaming white between cardinal bricks newly laid. A bell rings and disturbs crows in weltering willow boughs.

It's my father's temple, though he'd say a church belongs to no man but to God.

The last time I'd seen him preach a sermon was the August morning of the day I left home. He stood in the pulpit of a square frame building roofed with tin sheets. The sun flared off and scorched the tin, and dirt daubers pinged and bounced upward against it. He spread his strong arms wide and raised eyes the color of blueberries heavenward.

"Hear ye, hear ye, my people," he called out as always when he began a service. "The Lord is in this holy place."

He was a large man, heavy of bone, physical, his face full, the flesh itself weighty. His lank brown hair never seemed completely under control, and he constantly wiped it back from his tanned brow. He crowded the pulpit when he spoke as if it were a barrier placed in his path. He wanted to get at his congregation, grip them by their spiritual throats, force feed them on the richness of the Holy Word.

Yet his voice had many ranges. He might whisper in a fashion that needed no electronic assistance to carry it to the rear of the sanctuary. He'd next shout so loudly that babies woke and cried. He'd whine, plead, weep as well as sing in a rumbling bass baritone. Standing above us he often seemed the captain on a ship's deck ordering us to sail a course that would carry us across perilous seas to salvation.

"Don't call it *sanctuary,*" he told me. "It's *nave,* and it comes from the Latin *navis,* which means 'ship' or 'vessel.' We are all on life's journey."

We still lived in Tobaccoton, a sun-smacked formless town that had three galvanized warehouses for auctioning the coarse, torpid leaf growing from our enfeebled soil. Tobacco gave itself to heat and the pillaging sun. Field hands working rows sweated, drooped, and faltered, but tobacco luxuriated—as languorously female as oiled women unfolding themselves to the midday rays on a smitten July beach.

"Straighten your tie," my father told me. I was eight, and he'd looped and tightened the tie on me himself. We hiked a narrow blacktop road between dry ditches clogged with briars, poison oak, and bull thistles. Grasshoppers sprang around us. Locusts chirred, the sound moving over flat, cooked pastures like rolling waves.

We'd already knocked on most every door in town, including the homes of blacks who dropped nickels and dimes in the painted sheet-metal receptacle shaped like a miniature church that my father carried. He'd made it himself using snips and rivets. Coins clinked dully when swallowed by the slit. The roof could be unscrewed to dump out money.

We walked dusty lanes to the abject houses, many unpainted, the sidings pearly, a few boxlike with flues poking up at their centers. Hounds circled and barked at us. Despite its being a weekday and the summer sun's boiling down high and white, we wore go-to-meeting dark wool suits that itched even during cold weather. We kept our hair combed.

"Carry the Word reverently with both hands as you would with any precious belonging," my father instructed me. He meant my black leatherette-bound New Testament the cover of which I polished using a cotton rag lightly moistened with linseed oil.

We knocked on a screen door that had blobs of cotton pinned to it to scare off flies. The flies spiraled and resettled. A stout woman took shape back in the house, she wearing a pink smock and red flip-flops that smacked the rugless floor. Her face was deeply creased, her yellowish hair undone. She too sweated and swiped a hand at flies. Steam drifted from the kitchen. She'd been canning butterbeans and tomatoes.

"Hell's heat and Satan's fires can't stand against the Word of the Lord" my father said. The woman stared at him and me. Her name was Mrs. Bertha Stokes. I smiled big the way my father had taught me. We removed our hats.

Mrs. Stokes hurried back to the kitchen to switch off her stove and bring us jelly glasses of minty iced tea. My father and I sat on her porch swing. Soles of his black high-top shoes rasped the floor. The woman had work piled up but gave us of her time.

"Let us rejoice in the day the Lord has made," my father said and nodded to me.

I stood and sang "Jesus Loves Me."

Hoarded coins from a Mason jar hidden on a shelf of Mrs. Stoke's kitchen cabinet clinked slowly into the sheet-metal church I held to her. My father had taught me to count using pennies, nickels, and dimes spread out on boards of our rickety, coon-grape-entangled back porch after what he liked to call our missionary journeys.

Cars and pickups wind into the Temple of Zion's paved parking lot. A washed-and-wet combed suited youth directs me to a space beneath a hackberry tree's pale shade. Before leaving Myrtle Beach, I owned a madras sport coat but no tie. I bought one from a Dollar General in Rocky Mount, the cost seventy-five cents plus N.C. tax. The mishmash of colors resemble eggs smashed on the green felt of a pool table. I am in style.

Believers gather about on grass and church steps—men and women worn by labor, hardship, loss. Lacking among them is the fragrant gleam of money. Even the children seem serious and to sense the struggle ahead that life has waiting.

Their parents are what my father calls salt of the earth—lintheads, tillers of soil, jackleg carpenters and electricians, possessors of wary eyes that have looked deep into need and despair. The people sense I'm not one of them. Eyes weigh an alien in their midst.

By the time I reached eleven, my father'd wheedled and begged enough money to build his first church—a board-and-batten building with a small belfry, the interior stark, the pews wooden benches hammered together from raw lumber, a wood-burning iron stove at the center of the nave, its smokestack stuck through the roof. He named the church Zion. He'd drawn the plans on pages torn from the spiral notebook I carried to school.

"Go to Mr. Whitley and loan his wheelbarrow," he'd ordered me during construction. He'd stripped to the waist and wore a red, billed cap. He wanted people to see him sawing, pounding, and hoeing furrows in concrete for the front walk. His sweat glistened like a beacon.

"Don't want to," I said. We were always loaning from Mr. Whitley, the freight agent for the N&W. Mr.

Whitley didn't like to be borrowed from. He kept his tools in order by hanging them from pegs in his clean backyard workshop.

"It's not what you want, but what God wants of you," my father said.

"Mr. Whitley knows we broke his ladder," I said.

"We didn't hide that particular fact from him," my father said. He hammered bent nails straight to use again.

"You never told him neither."

"Git," he said.

We were always borrowing. He drew my mother into it. She felt shamed. I'd see her take a breath before leaving the house and crossing next door to our neighbors for a cup of sugar or sifter of biscuit flour. When my father organized a clothing drive for flood victims at Massies Mill, he told her to pick a few things for herself and me to wear from piles sorted in our yard.

"You're doing the Lord's work," he said. "Nobody will fault you for wanting to appear neat and properly turned out in His cause."

"What if somebody recognizes what I have on is their gift to Massies Mill?" she asked.

"You can turn the collar or change the buttons," he said.

She obeyed and sewed to disguise. No one ever accused her of wearing others' clothes, but she stayed fearful of it. I'd seen her eyes grow tearful while she pulled at a sleeve or adjusted a skirt over her lean hips.

She was a slight woman, a round pretty face, her hair strawberry blond and seemingly too abundant to belong to one so subdued. She'd been better born than my father, her people settled for generations in Halifax County where they owned a dairy farm.

At her parents' death, the farm went to her older broth-ers, and she received only a small inheritance. My father spent it on a Ford station wagon. She could letter well and painted ZION CHURCH on the front doors as well as a picture of a dove holding an olive twig in its beak.

I walk up the radiant concrete steps of Zion Temple. Three broad white double doors form the entrance. The two-story narthex is rose carpeted, and brass chandeliers with teardrop bulbs provide a genteel light. Another washed-and-scrubbed suited youth hands me a program. Large block print proclaims CELEBRATION!

"Sideshow," I say.

"Huh?" the youth asks, unsure. Sandy down grows above his mouth, and on his lapel he wears a small gold pin shaped like a wire fish. As I pass, I think of the difference in this resplendent temple and that first church my father built—bleak, unadorned, sunlight tracing grains of pine boards so unseasoned they still bled resin. Wind rattled and banged the roof, and during a hard rain my father had to shout to be heard above the drumming tin.

Before he received the call, he had been a carpenter. He'd arrive home and swoop me up in his arms while coated with golden dust from his saw. He smelled of pine, oak, walnut, cedar. I loved to hold to the hammer he wore in loops of his overalls.

He laughed and swung me about. He lifted my mother and kissed her. Fridays he drank beer with friends at the Dew Drop Inn beside the river. He never came home mean, though he did loud, and he'd perform a foot-stomping dance that shook the few pieces of good china my mother kept in the cherry glass-front cabinet he built for her.

He received the Call while hanging new gutters on the Dark Leaf Warehouse. The late summer afternoon was quiet and still, and he swore no cloud crossed the sky. As he climbed an aluminum ladder, lightning struck the roof and ran across it like a ball of white rolling fire.

Electric shock burned his fingers and soles of his shoes. He started sliding off and would've fallen had he not been able to hook the hammer's claw into a ladder rung. Members of the Howell County Volunteer Fire Department brought him down. For three days his mind stayed confused, and he uttered words that had no meaning for my mother or me.

"The road to Damascus," he said, the first sense he made as he sat barefooted on the back porch, his shirt off so his skin would catch the coolness drifting in with dusk. "I've felt the almighty and irresistible power of the Lord."

No longer did he drink with fellow workers on Friday evening, and he softened his rowdy language. He also stopped doing the dance. He'd gaze for long spells out windows and not hear my mother when she spoke.

He entered the Searchlight Bible College in High Point, wore black preacher suits, and carried a Bible even just walking into a grocery store to buy a dozen slices of baloney. He quit the college before the semester finished.

"You either hear the word of God in pumping of your blood or you don't," he told my mother. "No amount of classroom teaching changes that."

We returned to Tobaccoton and started raising funds, the times I'd go with him to knock on doors and sing "Jesus Loves Me" after which I held out the sheet-metal church for coins. He'd preach anyplace he believed the Word might take seed—a revival where he stood on a tree stump, Saturday nights in the parking lot of the Dew Drop Inn, at the livestock market shouting his message over the bawling of cattle who sensed death and walled their sad eyes.

When he'd collected five thousand dollars, he persuaded a kindly old farmer named Angus Yancey to sell two acres of land south of town in exchange for a 6 percent note. The note never got paid. Each year Mr. Yancey asked about his interest, and my father told him it was compounding.

Mr. Yancey died when his plow point hooked a vein of granite while he prepared ground for sowing wheat. The John Deere tractor pulled backwards on top itself and him. My father preached the funeral service and comforted the widow with repeated visits. She tore up the note.

He built the church by stretching every dollar into the value of two or three. He'd never spend a dime if he could garner it by borrowing or beseeching. That's why he'd send me to Mr. Whitley for tools and the wheelbarrow. He shamed people into giving of their time and money. The church rose in fits and starts. A bell once used to call hands from the fields rang in the small white steeple. I pulled the rope, the yellow hemp skinning my fingers.

The carnival arrived as it did every spring, a ragtag traveling show that had one elephant and a dried-up whale children could climb over and stand in the propped-open mouth of to get their pictures snapped.

The carnies raised the tents, booths, and brightly painted rides in a pasture across the road from the church property. My father went to Carrington Epes, Tobaccoton's banker, who owned the land and a great deal more of Howell County.

"There's gambling and girlie shows," my father said. "All

day and half the night we hear wheels of chance spinning and the hootchie-kootchie music. Can't hold prayer and fellowship meetings for the racket."

"And I can't break a contract," Mr. Epes said, he what my father called a Christmas Christian and di-luted Episcopalian. He drove a Cadillac car and had a daughter named Linda Lee, the raven-haired Tobacco Queen all the older boys loved—me too, though never admitted, hardly even to myself, believing my feelings about her sinful.

What infuriated my father most was the carnival operating Sunday afternoon. It was my job to clean up after the two-hour morning church service by collecting bulletins he'd typed and mimeographed on a secondhand machine that often broke down as well as sweeping up under the pews and switching off lights.

He sat in what he called his study, an unpainted, plywood cubicle, his jacket hung over his chair, his tie loose, his heavy legs sprawled out, blood in his face. He heard shouts of the barkers and music from the Ferris wheel and the whirling, flashing rides.

"Abomination upon abomination," he cried and swept an arm around him as if to clear the earth of corruption.

He strode from the church and across the road. I hurried after him. When angry, he walked with his palms swinging backward instead of turned to his sides. He waved me away, and I hung back.

Pickups had parked on the orchard grass. Crowds gathered and milled among booths and tents. The smells of cotton candy, sizzling hot dogs, and saltwater taffy mixed in my nose. Bright newly spread sawdust felt soft underfoot. A calliope shot steam from its silver pipes. Girls shrieked as the Ferris wheel spun them up into sunlight.

Scarlet banners displayed the Alligator Boy, the Borneo Fire Eater, and Half Man–Half Woman, a figure wearing a tuxedo along one side of their body, a wedding gown on the other, the face split forehead through the chin, a golden-haired maiden with ringlets to the left, a black-haired and mustached dandy right.

The hootchie-kootchie music sounded from metal loudspeakers set on a platform, and a barker shouted the show was about to begin for Fatima, who'd perform the dance of the seven veils. She stood swiveling her knees and hips, her gauzy harem clothes revealing her brassiere, panties, and meaty legs.

Her eyelids were darkened, her cheeks rouged. She chewed gum and looked out over the crowd as if thinking about something far away. Only men stood gawking. The women knew to keep a distance from that tent.

"Sultans have wept over her," the barker hollered. "Kings have left their thrones. The president of a South American nation jumped off a drawbridge into the sea."

The barker held a bamboo cane and rapped it against the platform's floor to the music's beat. He wore a red fez and dressed like Aladdin. Fatima raised her arms over her head and showed her rear view. Men whistled and hooted. She turned and again stared over them, seeing what?

My father climbed to the platform, crossed to her, and took her by the wrist to drag her down. He kicked over a loudspeaker, which on its side continued the snaky Arabian music.

"Cast down your eyes," my father called to the men. "You defile womanhood this holy day. Seek the Lord's grace."

They backed off chastened. Fatima cursed and struggled,

and the barker, a brawny, dark-complected man, jabbed his cane at my father's stomach. My father with a short straight punch knocked him flat to the platform.

Fatima screamed, twisted loose, and ran into the tent. The barker scrambled up, backed away, and hit my father over the head with the cane so hard it broke. My father caught him one-handed by the throat. The barker sank to his knees, his arms flopping like wings of a beheaded goose. His eyes bulged, and his false teeth worked loose from his gasping mouth and fell to the platform.

My father might've choked him dead had not a sheriff's deputy named Roy Ripley climbed the platform to stop him. When released, the barker pitched forward and vomited. Roy drove my father away in a brown-and-tan police cruiser.

He wasn't charged. Judge Pickney heard evidence that Fatima dropped all her veils during the show inside the tent, and he declared stripping illegal in Howell County. My father walked home at dark and crossed into his bedroom without speaking to my mother or me. He refused dinner.

I peeked in at him. He slumped on his knees, his hands clasped, his forehead resting on the quilted comforter kept back from the flood relief supplies sent to Massies Mill.

I felt proud. He'd done a crazy thing but shown himself to be brave and manly. Word about him traveled. At school I'd been treated by some pupils as a freak because I was the son of what they considered to be an unordained, redneck preacher, but now they eyed me differently—not so much with respect but alarm that I of his blood and genes might erupt if aroused.

My father continued to feel guilt. At the Wednesday service—the carnival had packed up and left—he proclaimed his remorse and repentance.

"Like Cain I've lifted my hand against my fellow man," he cried out. "I ask the Lord's mercy and removal of the blackness that Satan has implanted within me."

Yet after the service he ate three chicken drumsticks and two helpings of whipped potatoes and gravy. I caught him looking out the window toward the pasture where the carnival had been. Cotton-candy cones, ticket stubs, and Dixie cups lay strewn over sawdust and trampled grass. The smile stole onto his face and twitched till he realized I was seeing.

"Who can stand before the righteousness of the Almighty?" he asked, quickly solemn. "Let us clean up after the disorder left by Satan's deceived."

There are also three entrances from the narthex to the nave. I don't wait for an usher to lead me to a seat. There is little chance I'll be recognized, but I slip in along the wall and sit at the far end of the rear pew. Red velveteen cushions soften it.

Racked red hymnals and Bibles are embossed with gold lettering. No cardboard fans picturing a pretty Jesus are here supplied by the Daubenspeck Funeral Home. No flies or dirt daubers. Air-conditioned breezes flow from corners of the nave and flutter white ribbons tied to the grates.

A woman wearing a white vestment plays the organ. Like a sunburst its pipes rise to the ceiling behind the oak pulpit holding a brass lamp, the great Bible, and three microphones.

I remember the Tobaccoton organ. My father'd salvaged it from a barn and repaired it himself, and my mother had to pump it with both feet as she played. The organ wheezed like a wind-broke mule.

The Zion Church in Tobaccoton never prospered. Many Sundays less than fifteen people sat on our rough pews. There was no hope the congregation could ever support my father and mother. They went to work at the shoe factory. My father attempted to spread the Word among fellow workers during the lunch break. His message was hard and unyielding.

"The Book of Judgment," he preached. "You may think your sins trifling, a small lie here, a few cents cheated there, but they are all marked down, and the weight of them on that final day will drag you down to eternal perdition where the winds of darkness howl eternally and flames are quenched not."

Mainline church people avoided him—those he termed the Easy Episcopalians, the Muddled Methodists, the Braying Baptists. Howell County had no Catholics or Jews. Zion Church was never invited to participate in any of the interdenominational services at Christmas or Easter. My father's face became like a man's who'd been long treading into a cold blast.

During the spring I wanted to go out for track, but I would've had to quit my after-school job on the loading docks at the Southern State Co-op.

"We need the money," he said. "Remember the longest race of all is across the finish line to salvation."

He wanted and expected me to follow in his ministerial footsteps.

•   •   •

The brass collection plates on the alter table catch the gleam from bulbs of candlestick chandeliers. Sunlight is tinted blue and red as it filters through stained glass windows. Christ passes bread and fish to the uplifted faces of the hungry multitude. The hymn being played is "I Come to the Garden Alone."

I think of my mother.

She tended a small garden in the backyard, worked it when she came home from the shoe factory, a few rows of beans, Irish potatoes, Big Boy tomatoes, turnip greens, okra. She owned no plow or Rototiller. I forked up the ground for her after the first kill frost. Virginia's winter freezes crumbled the red soil and made spring planting easier.

She became quieter with the years. Sometimes I realized I wasn't hearing her voice as much as reading her lips. Playing the organ became difficult for her. Arthritis transformed her small worn hands into partial fists. The organ often squawked or shrieked.

I found her on a humid Fourth of July afternoon. She lay among rows of her garden. She'd been picking snaps and quarter filled a galvanized bucket. She clutched a pod in her fingers as if able to carry it wherever she went, and where she went was to death.

"Woman is the glory of man," my father preached in a blowing shower that flapped scallops of Daubenspeck's canvas canopy. "And her love is beyond riches."

Mourners came chiefly from the shoe factory. I thought that if he'd remained a carpenter and provided better for her, my mother wouldn't have died so early and forlorn.

Not that my father didn't honestly suffer her loss, but he

truly worshiped the unseen more than anything alive and devoted under his own roof.

The choir, wearing red vestments with white collars, appears, the members singing as they file from both sides of the nave into tiers of seats on a platform above and behind the pulpit. In the front row children, hymnals lifted high, round their mouths to fit words, voices piercingly innocent. They sing "Jesus Loves Me." I find myself lip-synching.

During months after my mother's funeral, my father for a time increasingly lost his way. He stood in the pulpit the Sunday after Easter and became confused and unable to finish a sermon on The Upper Room. He sat on our back porch and stared at the unplanted garden. More and more I did the cooking.

He'd always visited the hospital. Not all patients welcomed him. He got to Carrington Epes, the banker who'd rented land to the carnival.

Mr. Epes had bone cancer and wasted away. He feared death. My father sat daily by the bed and read from Psalms, Romans, Revelations. Mr. Epes suffered periods of confusion, and his two sons and daughter, Linda Lee, tried to bar my father from the room.

After Mr. Epes died, his children were outraged when my father came forward with a check for $75,000 payable to Zion Church. They sued to force a return of the money to the estate.

A nurse testified she'd seen my father hold a pen in Mr. Epes's hand. She couldn't be certain about a check being signed. My father stated he'd merely helped the banker put his name to a stock proxy. A specialist from the State

Crime Lab examined the check. Troubled by the wobbly signature, he still couldn't state positively it wasn't genuine.

"I take an oath here before God I've done nothing wrong," my father swore from the witness stand.

Mr. Epes's family settled out of court. Zion's Church received $37,500 and the payment of legal fees. At the end of the day my father sat in his study, the new check centered on the desk he'd made from scrap lumber. The summer evening was soggily humid, the air seeming to have grown heavy, and he'd removed his jacket and shirt. His sweaty arms glistened.

"Come sit," he said to me. He switched on the electric fan. He'd built shelves for the study, but they were yet not half filled, and that mostly with religious tracts and articles he'd scissored from newspapers to use in sermons. I glimpsed a headline: DEAD YOUTH BROUGHT BACK TO LIFE BY PRAYER.

"I'm sorry you had to hear those things charged against me in that courtroom," he said. "Happy your mother couldn't. What you need to remember, son, what I've come to find out, is there's a war going on for the soul of this country, and God's people are losing. They're losing because they won't stand up and fight the enemy on his own terms. Well I've learned something, and I'll fight them to the wall."

I never told him what I found that Saturday December morning when I burned trash in the wire incinerator behind the church. Fire uncurled a balled-up sheet of mimeograph paper from his office. I snatched it from the flames. The signature had been copied a dozen times on both sides, the ink black, the letters spidery: *Carrington J. Epes.*

Monday while he repaired the pull rope of the bell that called so few to Zion Church, I left home and Tobaccoton.

I watch my father as he enters from a carved Gothic door at the front of the nave. He mounts steps to the pulpit and lays sermon notes on it. He sits in one of the three red-cushioned thronelike chairs. He crosses his heavy legs. He wears no vestment, just a dark suit, but it isn't rumpled and fits him well. Perhaps he now has a tailor.

He has changed during the eleven years since I've been away. I served a hitch in the army, broke up a short marriage, and now own a TV repair store in South Myrtle Beach. For a time I received letters that followed me around the country. He wrote, "I mean to build a church for the people, a temple where the soul of common man can find refreshment, balm, and salvation."

While repairing a Zenith power pack, I first spotted him on the screen, an early morning time slot, his arms lifted and spread, his mouth pronouncing a benediction.

Later I read an account in the *Charlotte Observer* about his growing ministry. He'd apparently taken the Epes money first to buy radio time. As an audience grew, he'd begun appearing on the local tube, his telecast named *The Zion Hour.* I occasionally caught the show.

Over the years his delivery had improved and his message softened. He preached what the mainline churches defined as a heretical doctrine:

"Christ is among us this very moment," he said. "He could be standing beside you at work, sitting next to you on the bus, or coming around the next corner. He will not appear threatening among thunder and lightning and bring terror to the world. He will knock gently at your door and break bread at your table. Be ready to place your hand in His for the walk through darkness to the dazzling light of eternal truth."

From the TV I heard his continued call for money to build Zion Temple. He displayed architects' sketches and used a red crayon to fill in the dollar thermometer drawn on white poster board. He implored, at one broadcast weeping, dropping to his knees, holding out his arms as if waiting for them to be filled.

When I heard an announcement of the temple's dedication, I drove up from Myrtle Beach in my van. I sit in the pew watching my father, who seems rounded now, all edges gone. His cheeks have filled out but not sagged. His once unruly pale brown hair has thinned and become obedient to his scalp's contours.

The organist strikes the hour. The choir sings "Blessed Be the Tie That Binds." Ushers have seen to it the pews are uniformly filled. My father stands and raises those hands that he so ably put to work using hammer, chisel, and saw.

"Hear ye, hear ye, my people," he calls out. "The Lord is in this holy place."

His voice is a trained and fertile bass baritone now, a near musical coaxing to scatter the seeds of belief. His benign smile seems a dispensation. For an instant I worry he sees me. His eyes move on.

"The next person you encounter on the street," he intones, "may be our Savior who has come to bring surcease of pain caused by the heavy yoke this earthly life has laid upon your backs."

I watch these pinched and hungering people. He has learned well. His voice is balm, and they believe. Their faces lift and are made lustrous by hope and trust. His words salve their wounded spirits. He lightens their loads, and they straighten as grass rises from the weight of a departed foot.

While the choir sings "Amazing Grace," I slip from the pew and through the door into the narthex. An usher gives me a questioning look. I wink at him.

I walk down the steps and among dusty parked cars and pickups to the hackberry tree and my van. Voices of the choir and congregation surge with the swelling organ, a pulsating comber of joy and aspiration that becomes phased in with the chirring of locusts—shrill cries expanding under the sun's unrelenting brightness. I feel blinded and lightheaded and wish I could sing.

PLACE

The cool April morning the white van, customized on an International chassis, stopped at Tobaccoton's post office, I'd just walked out carrying Saturday's mail. The van had a large blue acorn painted on its side. Heavy animals clomped around back there. I knew the scent of horses.

"Looking for Route 717," the driver said, a young man, tanned, long blond hair, his khaki safari shirt open three buttons down the front and exposing chest.

"Route 717," I repeated, frowned, and tried to fix the location of what had to be a back road.

"Got off the track somewhere," he said and laid a map over the steering wheel. The cab had oxblood-colored leather seats, air-conditioning, and an extensive tape deck.

"Hold me your map," I said.

He dipped a finger onto a thin-lined secondary route that wound among farms in the southwest end of Howell County bordering the Falling River. I studied the pencilled X as I pictured the area.

"Old McGilly place," I said.

It'd been for sale—the once magnificent white brick house unoccupied a dozen years since Miss Bess McGilly fell down the porch steps and had to be situated by her nephew at Lynchburg's Westminster Canterbury. He put the place on the market a week after Miss Bess gave up the ghost.

"How about pointing me?" the driver asked.

He talked not countrified Virginian like Howell Countians, even schoolteachers, of which I was one. I used two dialects, the first local, the second for when visiting Tidewater cities and points north.

He drove away, and I walked home. I lived with my father in a gabled house built by his grandfather in the 1870s. The grandfather had been a United States ambassador to Chile. The place was much too large for us, and winters we closed the upstairs to save heat. Mantels held clocks no longer wound. The ambassador's statesmanlike portrait commanded the parlor. So much for our familial glory.

Lace doilies I washed and starched by hand protected arms of dowdy, bow-legged Victorian chairs. Our furniture had a weariness about it, and because of a leaky basement the house smelled of mildew from summer's heat to first frost.

Daddy managed the Southern States mill. When he walked home that evening at five-thirty I asked whether he knew of anything happening out at the McGilly place. He told me the word was it'd been bought by a man from Michigan with a thirst for land.

"Appreciate you keeping me informed," I said.

"Didn't know you had a mind set on real estate," he said.

He'd served a single term in the General Assembly and had a picture of himself shaking hands with Winston Churchill snapped when the ex–prime minister toured Virginia. Shortly afterwards Daddy got mixed up in the massive resistance movement. As a result he lost the black vote at the polls and his elected office.

No longer could he orate in the amber grandeur of Thomas Jefferson's capitol building. Defeat brought comedown to a desk among the invasive, chaff-bloated haze thrown up by Southern States' vast, throbbing hammer mill. Essences of sweet feeds and cottonseed meal lingered about his clothes.

If not for Daddy, I'd have broken from Howell County. It'd fallen to me to look after him when Mama died of an arterial brain rupture that knocked her sideways while serving dinner and sent her canting to the wall, her face astonished. As she fell, she clutched the sideboard and pulled over her silver service.

I'd been to Longwood College, earned a primary-education degree, and now taught the third grade, but lying abed nights I envisioned myself a citizen of Richmond, Norfolk, or Virginia Beach living in my own decorated apartment, a swimming pool or ocean nearby, also theaters, music, art, and men who knew what the subjunctive mood was and how to use it.

At sixteen Daddy had given me a foal I named Mademoiselle. I brought Selle along slow, training her to halter and lead line, no saddle till a two-year-old. I daily talked to and laid hands on her. When I stuck carrots in a pocket, just the tips showing, she nuzzled me to search for them. I'd turn my body to tease her, and she circled me till she found one. Her eyes were purple-within-purple orbs. When I looked into them, I saw trust and devotion.

Before driving out to the McGilly place, I hosed off my red secondhand F-150 pickup bought to haul hay for Selle as well as to pull a two-horse trailer I used to carry her to local shows. I washed my hair, wore my best jeans, a new white blouse, and three dabs of perfume.

Disturbed dust settled along the lane leading to the McGilly house. In pasture gone sour and sprouting volunteer locust seedlings, I made out a lowboy, a yellow dozer, backhoe, and well-drilling equipment. I painted on lipstick and reset my pearl-colored Stetson before stepping to the ground.

Trucks, cement mixers, stacked lumber, copper pipes, buckets of paint, and new gutters circled the house. Workers tore down Virginia creeper and raised scaffolding. Hammers banged, saws shrilled, a fire burned, the flames fueled by scaly pine cabinets ripped from the old kitchen.

The van driver who'd stopped at the post office stood in shade of a water oak, a sprig of orchard grass clamped in his teeth, a straw hat tipped forward. Shirtless, his chest hair sun bleached, he wore shorts and Wellington boots.

"Burn it," he ordered two men carrying out a pea-green sofa moths had feasted on.

"Well you found the place," I said and figured him to be the overseer for the new owner.

He stared, not sure of me.

"Gave you directions in town," I said. "You really got people humping it 'round here."

"Oh yeah," he said. "Going to be changes made."

"Owner must own a bank or two. Who he?"

"Fellow name of Gaston Farley."

"I'm Mimi. What's your handle?"

"Gaston Farley," he said and shouted at a worker carrying a coil of electrical wire wrapped around his body like a boa constrictor.

"How come you needed directions to find this place when you'd already bought it?" I asked.

"Flew in the first time. Landed in the pasture. Price was

right and made a purchase on the spot. Now something I can do for you or are you just nosy by nature?"

Yankee manners, I thought. Or lack of them.

"Wanted to see your horses," I said, thinking I should switch into my upper-level speech pattern.

"The paddock," he said and didn't offer to show me but pointed.

I crossed through an orchard planted in gaunt, cedar-blighted peach, apple, and pear trees. None bore fruit. A wagon road led to the paddock. Posts and rails gleamed newness. Carpenters framed what looked to become a stable near where a ramshackle farm equipment shed had been razed.

The paddock contained four horses, and at sight of them my breath came short. We locals rode western, a cowboy style, mounting sure-footed, short-coupled quarter horses. These beauties I stared at were long-legged, sleek, extended—all thoroughbreds sixteen hands or better, fit, lean, stopping their milling to watch me.

The arched-necked dominant animal paraded a lustrous black coat and imperial bearing. He detached himself from the others to advance several steps toward the fence. He snorted, tossed his head, and raked a hoof across the ground, raising reddish dust. Black Beauty resurrected, I thought. I'd grown up on the book and read it to tatters.

I returned to the house. Mr. Gaston Farley was not to be seen. One thing for sure. I had to know a man who flew in by plane and owned such horses.

The last Friday in May after school let out, I drove to Acorn Farm. I'd tried phoning and found the number unlisted. No Stetson or western garb this time, but my only pair of jodhpurs, a ratcatcher, earrings, and a red hair band.

The repainted house dazzled from its grassy knoll. Verandas had been restored, the sagging shutters pulled down and replaced, a new roof installed.

The four-car garage with servants' quarters above rose over the site of a demolished chinked tobacco barn. The white stable had dark green trim around doors and windows. A copper stallion, nose pointed to windward, topped the louvered ventilation spire.

Gaston cantered the black horse in a sandy ring adjoining the paddock. The two were so closely joined and synchronized that I thought *centaur.* Hooves drummed a beat to effortless grace.

Gaston reined the gelding, and turned him to the first of three jumps set at a height of four feet or so at the center of the ring. Horse and rider curved over negligently, indifferently, ho-hum, such a boring day. I realized my mouth had started to fall open.

Gaston drew the animal to a walk. As they passed, they eyed me.

"Something?" he asked.

"Use a stable hand? I work cheap—for rides."

"These aren't local cow ponies," he said.

"That's a sonofabitch remark," I said, ready to turn and leave.

"You're hired," he said and smiled over lovely strong male teeth.

Starting that morning, I slung manure into a spreader drawn by a John Deere tractor through the alleyway between stalls. I grained the horses, watered them, washed them, and heaved hay bales to fill feed racks. I cleaned hooves, combed manes, and pulled tongues to thrust worm pills so deep into throats the animals couldn't spit them up.

The black was Midnight Baron. During the first week I moved nervously about him, but despite his tossing head and menacing snorts, he quieted when I laid fingers along his muscled neck.

"All an act," Gaston said as we watched the Baron parade among mares of his domain. "Equine nostalgia."

"Seems a waste he can't stand stud," I said.

"A killer otherwise."

Gaston allowed me to ride the third week, not the Baron, but a bay named Felicia Delicia. Shown as a handy hunter, she'd won a barrel of trophies. He fitted her with an English saddle and a snaffle bit. Under me she felt tightly strung. Divining my insecurity, her sideways buck left me sprawled in dust.

"Got a long way to go, baby," Gaston said. He caught the mare, attached her to a lunge line, and gave me a leg up. As she circled him, he called instructions.

"Move forward in the saddle, but don't stiffen. Picture a horizontal drop from your head to your shoulders and down through your hips to your heels. Keep your head up. Think of yourself as a duchess, not a cowhand."

He bolted a full-length steel mirror to the north side of the stable so I could compare my seat to equitation photographs in books kept on the office shelf.

He didn't permit me to ride the Baron till early August. By then the horse and I had an earth-bound relationship. When I climbed from the mounting block into the saddle,

I felt ten feet off the ground, and as I first trotted and then cantered him around the ring, I sensed the immense but controlled strength between my legs.

"All right, take him over the oxer," Gaston ordered. "And don't look down at it."

By then I'd gone English and been working using a cavaletti and low jumps with Felicia Delicia. The Baron moved disdainfully toward the three-and-a-half-foot oxer, such an insultingly small barrier to him, but as he gathered and sprang I felt his soaring power. We left this earth, and for an instant I believed we'd never come down. I didn't want to.

"God, I loved that," I shouted as I reined the Baron to Gaston, who stood with arms resting on the fence. I dismounted, hugged the Baron's neck, looked into his eyes, their golden brown bottomless depths. "Like a religious experience."

"You one of these Pentecostals and know about religious experiences, do you?"

"I'm a Methodist."

"Read somewhere a Methodist is just a Baptist who can read."

"Your bastard nature's showing again," I said.

"Why you're catching on real well," he said.

During a thunderstorm, Gaston led me into his house. The carpenters, electricians, plumbers had at last finished. He'd hired a black man named Richard Doggins and his wife, Loris, to cook and keep up the place. They lived over the garage.

The large, high-ceiling rooms were furnished not with pine or southern-crafted antiques but European-style cabinets, inlaid secretaries, regal high-back chairs. Peacocks emerged from weaves of Persian carpets, oil paintings of horses hung from walls, and the dining-room hunt board held salvers, goblets, and an enormous silver punch bowl etched with a coat of arms.

"Go on and ask," Gaston said as I leaned to peer at the coat of arms and made out a knight's helmeted head and lions rampant bounded by a long triangular shield. "You wonder about the money. I'll let you in on a dark secret. I'm Mafioso."

"Sure," I said but felt so impressed by the grandeur of the house's interior I would've believed almost anything.

I followed him to the library, the walnut-paneled walls holding bookshelves floor to ceiling. He drew down a photograph album and showed me a photograph of an elderly man wearing a white suit, panama hat, and black bow tie. Behind him on a lawn were fanback wicker chairs, a sundial, palm trees, and a glimpse of the sea.

"The former boss of all bosses, and my father. Trained as a doctor but never treated a patient because of his Midas touch. Everything turned to gold—real estate, stocks and bonds, foreign currency. You can spread the word among your curious brethren."

"I don't spread things about you or anything that goes on at Acorn. And they could be your brethren too."

"First time I catch you doing it, you're gone," he said.

He threw parties, yet none for "my brethren." Arriving guests did not drive pickup trucks. They stepped from expensive, carelessly treated sporty cars—elegantly turned-out women and handsome, vigorous men. They had flair and the snotty poise incubated by money.

Early September I hated being back at school and among

students, some who gave off urine odors and carried head lice. When I told Gaston I could no longer help regularly during the week but still hoped to work his horses whenever I had time, he shrugged. To his friends I suspected he called me his local-yokel stable hand.

I'd been neglecting Selle. She stood at the fence of my Uncle John's farm and looked forsaken. I loved her, but after the Baron beneath me her gentle nature made her feel a mount more suited for children. Her eyes charged betrayal.

Gaston surprised me when he phoned in mid-October and asked whether I'd like to go fox hunting. I believed he meant me to ride beside him, and my heart squeezed. No, Gaston needed help because Joe-boy, the black stable hand who'd replaced me, had come down with blood poison from spearing a foot with a pitchfork's prong.

I broke a date with Wilford Emory, whom I'd known from my high school days and who worked for the Soil Conservation Service. I told him I had flu, felt ashamed for lying, yet couldn't refuse Gaston. I'd never attended a hunt.

Since I'd be traveling as a groom, I wore Levi's, a flannel shirt, a leather jacket, rubber boots, and a cap. I pulled into Acorn Farm at four-thirty. Gaston had lowered the van's ramp, and we loaded Midnight Baron. After fastening the cross ties, I latched the butt bar.

We drove toward Richmond, our headlights pushing darkness before the van as Gaston played operatic tapes. His white stock and gold safety pin that secured its knot caught a glow from the lighted dashboard. I thought of English nobility.

At dawn he turned off the four-lane highway into a village called Lowland, then rolled past secluded estates and up a magnolia-lined lane to a white clubhouse. Linen-covered tables had been set on the lawn, and white-jacketed colored waiters laid out food and drink.

Riders nibbled ham biscuits and drank from proffered stirrup cups—the women haughtily poised in their black Meltons and canary breeches, the dashing men wearing scarlet, toppers, and carrying whips with staghorn handles. Horses' nostrils steamed into crisp morning air.

We unloaded the Baron. I held Gaston's hunt coat for him. Engraved fox heads decorated the buttons. People called to him, and he responded and tipped his topper to ladies who knew his name and bestowed smiles. He mounted and rode off with just a lift of his whip to me—a hell of a way to say thanks, but then I reminded myself I'd been brought along to replace Joe-boy.

The huntsman, a large, ruddy man riding a heavy Roman-nosed liver chestnut, arrived with the hounds, thirty or forty following him in a clotted pack. Several growled and bared their teeth, and he cracked his whip over them to quiet the fuss.

Astride a gleaming gray Arabian, the master approached—a slim, condescending presence who others made way for, male members raising their hats and wishing him good morning, the women dipping forward as if to the passage of royalty.

Riders closed about him as he called out announcements in an Anglicized voice—watch your footing, the location of the next meet, a breakfast to follow the chase. He nodded to the huntsman, who from a leather holster attached to his saddle drew a copper horn and sounded it. The excited hounds moved off after him across the lawn and through an opened gate to a frost-coated field and down toward willows bordering a crooked, glinting stream.

This early morning light appeared cleaner, purified, and reflected off scarlet, brass, and the rich gloss of the finest horses I'd ever seen. Could money refine the sun's rays?

I felt envy and sadness not to be among people riding out in such great beauty. I became fully conscious of my class status—a downstairs maid peeking into the palace window at exquisite dancers attending the splendid grand ball.

The chase lasted three hours. I sat in the van, walked around the stable, watched servants clear away linen cloths. I didn't have nerve to ask about using the clubhouse bathroom and relieved myself in the van.

When riders returned, grooms moved out to take the horses. Gaston rode beside a beautiful dark-haired woman who wore a shadbelly and lady's topper. They laughed, and she touched fingers to her lips and reached them to his.

Mud had splattered his boots. I exchanged Midnight Baron's bridle for a halter, removed his saddle, cleaned his hooves, rubbed him down, strapped on his blanket.

"Put a grey to ground and lost a red on the far side of the creek," Gaston said as he combed his hair in front of the van's side mirror. "Baron seemed a little gimpy at the end. Likely bruised the off-hind on gravel."

I checked the hoof a second time and found no injury. Possibly it wasn't the hoof but the shoulder. All that jumping of fences applied great pressure on ligaments, joints, bones. I loaded him. Gaston wiped his boots and strode off hatless toward the clubhouse and food. I'd had nothing to eat. Never thought to bring a sandwich. I hated him.

As he crossed the lawn, he hesitated and looked back. I must've appeared dejected and resentful.

"Come on," he said and gestured me to join him.

"Not going in there," I said.

"Oh yes you are," he said and returned. He gripped my elbow to guide me over the crunchy grass to the clubhouse entrance.

Inside, photographs of hounds, huntsmen, and past masters decorated walls. A glass-front showcase displayed silver trophies. A sumptuous breakfast buffet waited on long trestle tables, and blue flames burned under a battery of chaffing dishes.

At the bar Gaston ordered wine for the lady, meaning me, and a vodka martini for himself. The chilled Chardonnay tasted heavenly. As we drank, we circulated, and he introduced me as if I belonged. Despite my jeans, members treated me cordially. Several other women present were likewise casually dressed. Perhaps people considered me rich and horsily eccentric. I experienced the double high of wine and acceptance.

I ate fresh fruit, hot peppered sausage, eggs Benedict, Belgian waffles. Afterwards we thanked the hosts, a married couple named Kinslow, and Gaston, who'd not eaten much and was still drinking, asked me to drive.

Darkness settled in as we reached Acorn Farm. He and I put the Baron in his stall, watered, and fed him. As I turned from refastening the clasp on the oat bin, I bumped into Gaston. We kissed and didn't go to the house but settled on stacked bales of sweet-smelling alfalfa.

It was midnight before I drove the pickup home. I told my father, who'd worried and waited draped in his bathrobe, we'd had van trouble on the road.

Gaston hunted every weekend the weather permitted during the season. I bought a Melton and derby, and

Gaston allowed me to ride Felicia Delicia hilltopping as well as paid my capping fee. I became recognized by hunt club members, spoken to, and hats were lifted to me.

After chases Gaston liked his liquor. His room had a king-sized bed, elaborate French highboy, and an ornate mahogany armoire that held guns used to shoot dove, quail, and grouse. I left some of my things in his bathroom and closet.

Midnight Baron's gimpiness hadn't improved, though Gaston stopped riding him to allow time for healing. A vet's examination discovered no injury. We vanned the Baron to Charlottesville and an equine X-ray clinic. The specialist found a calcium buildup at the near shoulder. Each day I massaged that joint with a hot thin oil that sank deep.

March brought wind and freezing rain that shattered tree limbs and cut power. The hunt season over, Gaston was restless. When drinking, he became sexually playful. He emerged from the bathroom naked except for his boots, a topper, and a blue ribbon tied around what he called "my erect manhood." He pointed downward and asked, "How's that for a winner?"

With no explanation he flew to the West Indies. I remembered the tall aristocratic lady who'd touched fingers from her lips to his. Though unasked, I drove daily to check on the horses and make sure recovered Joe-boy did his job.

"He paying you?" Daddy asked, sitting before a fire he'd laid in the den that any time of year smelled of ashes. Except for the kitchen, all other rooms were drafty and cold. He'd given up tobacco but met some inner need by mouthing an empty briar pipe.

"I'm still learning and can ride anytime I want," I said knowing he wondered about Gaston and the fact Wilford Emory no longer phoned. Daddy gazed at me, yet inquired nothing further.

I hoped to have Midnight Baron fit by the time Gaston returned. The animal still possessed pride of power, though I continued to sense a slight hitch at his canter. Occasionally he dipped his head for no reason I could discover. Carelessness, I wondered, or pain?

Gaston came back tan as toast, his hair needing a cut. He decided to have a swimming pool installed at the side of the house. He'd purchased another horse, a black, heavy chested Hanoverian six-year-old that flowed like smoke over jumps. The Baron was turned out to pasture, again in hope a rest would cure whatever troubled him.

Gaston now invited me to his parties. I became acquainted with his friends, passed around canapés, sat at the dinner table, and attempted to converse wittily. I worked developing a third level of speech I termed "clipped profane sarcasm." I received certain knowing looks.

Occasionally I stayed nights. When Daddy asked about it, I told him the foals needed attention. Did he believe me? I couldn't be certain. He had a vacant way of looking past me and seeing what—my mother, his term in the General Assembly, a wrong turn taken, a dream passed by?

Finally summer, school dismissed, a bountiful time for horses and Gaston. He and I swam together, nights often stripping off sweaty clothes and flinging them to the pool's concrete apron. The turquoise water spotlighted from beneath gave our bodies the eerie appearance of floating greenish blue creatures from another planet.

•　　•　　•

lays swept past so quickly I felt myself in-
fter them as if I could snatch the minutes
e. I'd once thought September beautiful,
ıg brought somber misery. After only a
lt drained.

r I attended a mandatory and deadly
dull teachers conference in Fredericksburg. When I arrived
back, I quickly changed clothes and drove to Acorn Farm.
I needed air, space, and Gaston.

He wasn't at the house. Nor was Midnight Baron in the
pasture. I thought Gaston must've ordered Joe-boy to put
the horse up to have him shod or his teeth floated but
found the stall empty.

I spotted Loris at the kitchen door. She held a bucket of
seven-top greens picked from a garden she maintained. She
said Mr. Gaston and Joe-boy had driven a piece of machinery to the low grounds.

When I started across the pasture, I heard the shot. For
an instant, I stood wondering. Then I bolted. I climbed
fences and as I ran briars snagged my Levi's. I opened the
aluminum gate at the stand of long-leaf pines bordering
the cleared land and followed a dirt road to the low
grounds. Tire tracks and hoof prints had imprinted the soft
clay.

I heard the engine before I saw the yellow flash of the
backhoe. Gaston, carrying a shotgun, climbed the slope.

"What?" I asked and walked around him.

Joe-boy sat at the backhoe's controls. In a scrub patch of
land gone to weeds he piled red moist soil. A chain had
been wrapped around Midnight Baron's hind legs and
bolted to the machine's claw. The claw folded inward and
pulled the horse's limp body. Baron's tongue dragged

through dirt, and his shattered forehead was bloody gapped meat that left a trail of scarlet brilliance. He flopped bonelessly into his grave.

"Jesus, you didn't," I said.

"Latest X-rays show his condition inoperable. Not breeding stock and can't again be safely ridden."

"He trusted you, and you brought him down here and used a shotgun? You couldn't have paid a vet for a painless injection? You dump Baron in this shitty place."

"Death was quick and painless," he said. He carried the double breached across his arm as if on a grouse shoot.

"Just dumped like garbage. You couldn't have let him live and graze out his life?"

"Champs don't want to live crippled."

"How you know, you sonofabitch, he wouldn't still love the sunshine, the grass, the company of mares? Just jerked in that goddamn hole. No sheet or words over him."

"Better cool off with a swim," Gaston said. He strolled wide of me up toward the house.

Joe-boy used the backhoe to drop soil over the Baron. I ran past Gaston, climbed fences, yanked open the pickup's door. I wept, my eyes so overflowing that despite the sun my reaching home was a journey through a quaking, murky wetness of a land I'd never seemed to have known.

I didn't return to Acorn Farm the next morning or days immediately following. I taught school, did the cooking, washing, cleaned rooms, groomed Selle, and stopped breathing each time the phone rang. Surely I meant something to Gaston. He will, I thought, need and call me.

All callers asked for Daddy except the Reverend Thomas Cralle, our Methodist minister, who reminded me of the congregational breakfast held in the church's Fellowship Hall the third Sunday each month. Women were expected to provide food and drink.

Cool autumn nights after I finished the kitchen and grading homework, I sat with Daddy in our den. We commented on traded parts of the newspaper. Blowing leaves scraped down the roof and scratched at the windowpanes. Without appearing to, Daddy observed me. What did he expect to see?

I had to know about Gaston and drove toward Acorn Farm on a cold Saturday night. Before I reached the lane, sleet began to fall. I stopped short of the house. Windows were warmly lighted, and the water oak's limbs laid long pitching shadows over the glittering ice-speckled grass. I smelled smoke from the chimney and recognized a few parked cars. Gaston was throwing another party for imported friends.

Of course I'd been replaced. In Gaston's world, horses, houses, and people were. I backed off and returned home, driving carefully over the dark slippery pavement, the sleet rapping the windshield so hard I thought it might crack the glass.

"Going to bed early, aren't you?" my father asked when I told him goodnight and made for my room. The newspaper was spread across his lap.

"Been a day," I said.

ROLL CALL

People considered Uncle John a courtly dandy. He liked his seersuckers crisply fresh and in cooler weather never wore his suits without vests. During the coldest part of winter he became probably the last man in Richmond to fasten on dove gray spats.

He doffed a Homburg until Easter when he replaced it with a black banded Panama. The day the calendar officially announced fall's arrival he restored the Homburg. He owned a bamboo summer cane. The rest of the year he carried a malacca, which had a circular silver knob he kept polished.

"What's he ever done?" my Aunt Rose May asked. She wasn't Uncle John's sister but my mother's. Uncle John could claim no blood kin, being my grandmother Harriet's second husband.

"The Rutledges were prominent," my mother said. She was rounder than Aunt Rose May, her brown hair held less captive in nearly invisible nets.

"Whether the Rutledges were illustrious or not, he shouldn't continually expect to be waited on," Aunt Rose May said.

We lived in the house that'd belonged to Grandmother Harriet, built by her first husband, a leaf exporter, and located on Grove Avenue near Richmond's Battle Abbey.

As a boy I'd stared yearningly at the glass-enclosed displays of spurs, knives, guns, and battle flags as well as the great mural of mounted Robert E. Lee and his generals, whose names I could quickly recite.

Grandmother Harriet had shocked my mother and Aunt Rose May by slipping off one October morning and driving with Uncle John to Sea Island for a secret ceremony. She had a kind heart, though it beat irregularly, and eleven months later it gave way while she washed her white hair. My mother found her hanging on to the sink, strands of the hair tangled around a flowing faucet.

Grandmother Harriet had changed her will to leave her stocks and bonds to Uncle John, though my mother and Aunt Rose May received the house. Uncle John stayed on in the second-floor master bedroom. He appeared regularly at meals as if death had changed nothing. He was always gentlemanly, yet expected his laundry to continue to be washed and his room cleaned without making any financial contribution toward the house's upkeep.

It was a terrible time for my mother. She'd lost not only her mother but just before Christmas also my father, a Navy pilot, his body never recovered from the Atlantic. She ordered a headstone erected in the family plot, but his grave remained empty under the flowers she placed there.

She received his military insurance and a small pension, yet the rambling house required unending care. The cost of oil heat stayed high even when the third-floor rooms were closed tight. Mama and Aunt Rose May needed a man around who could use a hammer, saw, and wrench, the type of person my father had been. Uncle John's hands were long and tender, the nails well cared for and shiny as snail shells rubbed with spit.

After each meal, he liked a cigar, the scent of which lingered around the house and further upset Aunt Rose May.

"You never get it out," she complained. "It's in the rugs, the furniture, the walls."

Aunt Rose May hadn't married. She taught school and helped with house chores like vacuuming and washing and ironing the parlor curtains. She placed part of her salary each month in the porcelain Spode tureen on the dining-room sideboard. That fund was used for food and other expenses.

"If he won't contribute, he could at least come to the table on time," she complained.

Uncle John slept till eight-thirty each morning, bathed, and liked to be served a three-minute egg and a strip of bacon. He also expected the newspaper to be folded beside his plate on the table, though he didn't pay for the delivery. Mama bustled in from the kitchen to set food before him and struggled to control her exasperation.

"If he'd just hurry," she whispered to Aunt Rose May.

"You ought to confront him," Aunt Rose May said, her lips drawn tight and thin.

"Mother loved him dearly," Mama said. "We have to remember that."

When Uncle John finished breakfast, he lit his Corona, looked over the *Times-Dispatch,* and stood to make ready for his stroll downtown.

"You'd think like other men he'd have to be at his office by nine," Aunt Rose May said.

"The market doesn't open until ten," my mother said. We'd frequently heard him talking investments over the phone.

"A phone for which he also pays nothing," Aunt Rose

May said. Her resentment firmed and made her so brittle she might've shattered had she bumped a table or chair. "And what's he done with Mama's money? She would've wanted him to spend at least some of it on her house."

Despite his age, Uncle John hadn't married till he courted Grandmother Harriet but lived with his aging mother, Alice Chadwell Rutledge, whom Aunt Rose May called "the last grande dame of that peculiar clan." He cared for her during her sickly lingering years of pernicious anemia.

Uncle John was always kind to me, not playing ball or roughhousing like my father, whom I'd known till I was fourteen, but treating me in a much more adult fashion. He helped me write a paper for school on the Battle of Sayler's Creek, a bloody last-ditch fight and slaughter during what Grandmother Harriet had called the "War of Northern Aggression." I'd used the expression "rapacious blue bellies" in describing the overwhelming force of Yankee soldiers that overtook General Robert E. Lee's tattered Army of Virginia.

Uncle John was sitting in our den before the fire, the evening newspaper, which he also didn't pay for, opened to the financial page. He wore what people used to call a smoking jacket—gray with dark piping around the lapels and pockets.

"I don't think 'rapacious' is the word you want," he said. "There are always good and brave men on either side of any war, and when they die, they too leave wives and children who mourn them. Courage is the same in every breast."

"Were you a soldier?" I asked.

"For years I suffered from stomach ulcers," he said.

"They ran in the family, but in my youth I attempted to enlist first in the army, then the navy. The Rutledges had a military tradition. My grandfather was a bugle boy who sounded his battalion's charge when mighty Stonewall's foot cavalry broke and routed Hooker's right at Chancellorsville. His son a colonel riding beside Teddy Roosevelt up San Juan Hill. My father a captain of artillery with the AEF in France, and were it not for my physical disability I'd have been a West Point cadet."

On my birthday he gave me the bugle that had belonged to his grandfather Joseph Fortney Rutledge. He led me to the basement where he opened a steamer trunk stored close to the furnace to prevent mildew. He unwrapped the bugle from a gray flannel bag that had a faded yellow drawstring.

"Can you blow it?" I asked, thrilled and holding the instrument across my palms. Though it seemed too small and compact to signal battle commands, I thought it a wonderful gift. I prized even the dented bell, which Uncle John couldn't explain, but I liked to believe had been caused by a minnie ball during a howling advance that won victory for Stonewall and General Lee.

"Once I could," he said. "My lip's gone. You'll have to practice."

I did in our garage. I learned the military calls—assembly, mess, tattoo, taps, and of course the charge. Aunt Rose May made a face about the bugle, and my mother, who'd been teaching me piano, felt disappointed I didn't give more time to the Baldwin in our parlor.

I kept the bugle close at hand till I accepted the fact the instrument had a limited range no matter how hard I tried to extend it. Still it prepared my lip for me to take up the trumpet at John Marshall High and march in the band. I fitted the bugle back in the flannel bag and laid it among shirts in the bottom drawer of my dresser. On top was a framed photograph of my father in full dress naval uniform, his face smiling, behind him the white nose and canopy of a F-14.

Taxes drove Aunt Rose May to confront Uncle John about helping with expenses. A city reassessment increased the levy three hundred dollars annually. She clenched the bill the very moment Uncle John walked in the door Friday afternoon. He'd picked up the *News-Leader.*

"I'd like a word with you privately," she said, her face pale and hard as enamel. Behind her glasses, her green eyes appeared enlarged.

"Certainly, Rose May," he answered as he hung his Homburg on the oak hall rack and stuck his malacca in the brass umbrella stand. They walked to the den where she slid the mahogany doors shut. I listened with my right ear against the scrolled wood, but the doors were thick and heavy, and I could catch only snatches, mostly from Aunt Rose May whose voice became shrill.

"We're just two women trying to hold things together," she said. "And we need help."

"I apologize," Uncle John answered. "Please forgive . . . had no idea I was causing such distress . . . can be sure the situation will be rectified . . ."

Mama caught me listening and drew me into the hallway. She prodded me ahead of her into the dining room just in time, for Aunt Rose May opened the den doors and still clutched the reassessment bill. She marched past without a word and up the front steps.

Uncle John appeared more confused than disturbed. He

patted his hair the color of old ivory and tugged at his vest to draw out a wrinkle.

"Simply a misunderstanding I quickly intend to correct," he said to my mother.

"I didn't want this to happen," she said and turned her attention to the tea cart, where she'd been rearranging the china cups left by Grandmother Harriet.

"Consider it forgotten," Uncle John said and gave her the slow gentle smile that melted away her frettings.

I snuck into his room Saturday morning while my mother and Aunt Rose May grocery shopped. Uncle John had left the house, telling us he was walking downtown to check his office mail. Glancing about guiltily, I quietly slid open drawers of his chiffonier and found not only his spats but also two hairy pelts wrapped in tissue paper. Wigs. He wore wigs.

I looked at the stylish clothes in his closet where his trousers hung upside down from clips attached to padded wooden hangers. His polished black shoes had been precisely positioned on the floor. I smelled the odor of his cigars.

Back on the shelf under a battered Knox hat box I discovered a flat case that appeared to be made of fine antique walnut. Carefully I freed the brass latch and slowly uncovered glittering rows of cuff links—all sorts and sizes, some shaped like stars, moons, tennis rackets, golf clubs, porpoises, bluebirds, gargoyles, coins, watermelons, pistols, others made of gold and a few set with pearls, opals, rubies. The pairs rested in padded satiny slots that lined the case.

Though Uncle John always used links in his French cuffs, I didn't remember ever seeing him wear any of these ornate ones. A collection from his earlier days, I thought, or perhaps heirlooms that had belonged to the family Aunt Rose May called the "illustrious" Rutledges.

Quickly I closed the case, replaced it on the shelf, and slipped from the room. When Uncle John entered the house at noon, I eyed his hair to see if I could spot the wig. There seemed to be a faint coupling along the rear of his neck.

That evening before dinner, Aunt Rose May walked to the sideboard to deposit her weekly payment. She lifted the Spode tureen's lid, started to stick in her hand, and drew back. "What's this?" she asked. As she turned to my mother, she held up a sheaf of money bound by a rubber band. Puzzled, Mama shook her head and looked at Uncle John.

"Least I could do," he said and smiled.

Aunt Rose May became both pleased and embarrassed. She chattered during the meal and offered to bring Uncle John a second slice of chocolate chess pie, which he accepted. She made no face when he lit his cigar.

Weekly thereafter Uncle John left what Aunt Rose May called his "donation" in the Spode tureen.

"He's really an extremely generous man at heart," Aunt Rose May said.

The next time I sneaked into his room I'd stayed home from school on a blowing January Thursday because of a sore throat. Aunt Rose May was at work, Uncle John downtown at his office, and my mother had driven to the drugstore to fill a prescription. I again wanted to see those cuff links.

When I opened the case, several pairs were missing. He could be using them, I thought, yet that evening as he settled into his chair to read the paper, he wore ones I'd often seen him choose—silver ovals, his initials engraved in English script and nearly worn away.

"Are the cuff links Uncle John wears valuable?" I asked Aunt Rose May. She was finishing up at the kitchen sink.

"Old maybe but hardly precious," she said. "Why?"

"Just wondering," I said. "Do you think maybe he wears a wig?"

"Entirely his affair," she said, which meant she did know, and gave me a look. It was hard to stay ahead of Aunt Rose May.

Each Monday during the winter he continued to lay money in the Spode tureen. As a result, living became easier around the house despite cold northeast winds that seemed to find every crack or gap in the old house and caused it to creak. Seemingly endless rains flooded the James and turned it an ugly rampaging brown. For his birthday my mother baked Uncle John an angel food cake, and Aunt Rose May bought him a pair of Italian leather gloves.

Evenings Uncle John often received calls and slid closed the den's doors to do his talking. I answered the phone on a drizzling afternoon when he was still downtown.

"If you'll leave your name and number," I said to the man who'd asked for him. Mama had taught me to do that.

"Just tell him Vincent," the man said. "He'll know."

"And the number?" I asked.

"He's got it," Vincent said. "And tell him to hurry."

I told Uncle John as he was taking off his overcoat. It had raindrops lodged in the wool fabric. He hesitated before hanging it in the hall closet.

"All the world's in a rush to what end?" he asked.

The afternoon of a warming March day I snuck into his room a third time. He was still at work, and downstairs Mama and Aunt Rose May planted tulip bulbs in our window boxes. I unlatched the case. More empty slots. I searched the top of his chiffonier and in drawers and found no other cuff links.

On Friday morning during Easter break, I followed Uncle John when he left the house. I wanted to know where his office was and exactly what he did. I waited along the block on the other side of Grove Avenue.

At a few minutes after ten he passed, in no hurry, tipping his Panama hat to ladies, his cane's ferrule striking the sidewalk every second step. He wore no overcoat this sunny day, though he did have on the gloves Aunt Rose May had given him. He was still a distinguished looking man, tall, erect, and he made me feel that not even a hurricane or bomb could cause him to quicken his pace or move awkwardly.

He continued along Grove to Lombardy to Park. He paused and watched pigeons gathering to peck scratch corn somebody had thrown on the grass. He circled Monroe Park and entered Grace and Holy Trinity. I peeked through the church door into the vaulted blue space. There was no service. He simply sat, his Panama off, his gloved hands resting on his cane, and stared toward the chancel and the glimmering silver chalice on the spotlighted red altar.

He nearly saw me as he left along the aisle. I quickly knelt to the prayer bench and bowed my face into my hands. He passed by.

Uncle John continued through Monroe Park and then along Belvedere to the river where construction crews worked repairing the Lee Bridge. He leaned on his cane

and watched a crane swing steel buckets of concrete into an
excavation. The river's current, still high from spring rains,
swirled and hissed along the bank and against piers. Trucks
backed into the excavation to unload clanging I-beams. A
bucking jackhammer raised dust that hazed the sunshine.

He reset his hat and walked back along Belvedere to
Cary where he stopped before a brick antique shop and
looked in the window. He must've known somebody inside
because he raised a hand, stood a moment, a gloved palm
still turned upward. Slowly he let the hand down.

He moved on up toward Main. Before following, I
stopped at the shop. Its door was open, but I saw no one
back in the narrow dimness. The window displayed empty
wooden picture frames, a dusty cavalry scabbard, and a
painting curled at the edges of hunters jumping wild-eyed
horses over a stone fence as they chased hounds across a
straw-colored field.

Uncle John next walked Franklin Street to the lawn of
the state capitol. The sun, the church bells, the freshness of
the day had brought people from office buildings. They
lounged, stretched, and gazed at the limitless blue sky with
wonder that winter had retreated before a sweet-scented
spring.

He sat on a green bench along the maple-shaded path-
way and raised his hat to young matrons pushing baby car-
riages. They returned his smile. He brought out a cigar and
smoked it, recrossed his legs, and watched an irate mockingbird dive at a hustling squirrel.

He lowered his head. Why, I thought, he's having himself a snooze. He roused to look at his pocket watch. At
last, I thought, he's going to his office.

He walked again to Main and into Forrest, Hill, &

Dunne, a brokerage house, where he stood watching the sliding tape. He next entered an executive office at the rear of the noisy trading room. An elderly, dignified man stood from his desk. They talked. I pretended to read a research report on hospital stocks. When I glanced back, I saw the man shake his head.

I scooted out and waited at the far end of the building's marble corridor. Uncle John paused before the water cooler. He didn't drink but seemed undecided which way to move next. It was almost eleven-thirty. He had to be headed to work.

He walked from Main Street up to Franklin and the Richmond Public Library where he climbed the stone steps, removed his hat, and entered.

As I lingered, I hid myself behind a cream-tinted square column and display board on the library's porch. Book jackets flapped in a variable breeze. When Uncle John didn't come out, I sidled inside and peeped around the reading room. I spotted him sitting at a table near a sunny window. He'd laid his hat, gloves, and cane across a chair and held a book.

I pretended to read magazines, first *Time* and then in *Southern Living* an article about the planting and care of orchids, seeing the same line over and over, "The soil must be carefully prepared and nurtured." I kept my face covered and sneaked looks around the glossy pages.

At twelve-forty by the wall clock, Uncle John pushed from his chair to go to the men's room. I hurried to the book he'd left open. My eyes snatched up the line, " 'Let us cross over the river and rest in the shade of the trees.' " A librarian watched. I moved on among stacks.

Uncle John returned, sat, and again took up the book till one-thirty. He yawned and reached for his cane, gloves, and hat. He carried the book to the lady at the circulation desk, and they had a friendly whispered conversation.

He crossed Franklin Street to a sidewalk vendor who sold sandwiches and sodas from an umbrella-covered push-cart. Uncle John set his cane against a power pole to eat a hot dog. He held a paper napkin under it and maneuvered not to spill any mess on his clothes. He drank Coke from a can. He made the simple lunch seem leisurely, fashionable dining.

He glanced my way but didn't see me behind a Chevy parked alongside Linden Row. He wiped his mouth carefully before dropping the napkin into the plastic trash bag hanging from the vendor's cart. He spoke to the chef-hatted black man, who laughed and nodded.

Uncle John returned to the library where he picked up the book the lady had kept for him and sat in the same place. This time I pretended to read *Business Week*. On the cover large black letters printed against a red background asked, RECOVERY IN SIGHT?

Uncle John stayed seated till three forty-five. If he'd been reading, the print must've been fine or heavily footnoted because he rarely turned a page. Mostly he'd looked out the window in the direction of the river. After he put his book back on the shelf, he again spoke pleasantly to the lady at the circulation desk.

He walked out and strolled up Franklin and along Monument, passing Stuart, Lee, Davis, and Jackson. He turned down Shields Street to Grove and paused to stoop and pick a wild violet at the edge of a lawn held up by a concrete retaining wall. He drew the violet into his lapel. Reaching our house, he lifted the paper from the porch and entered at exactly five o'clock.

As he sat in his chair reading before dinner, I joined him. The banjo clock on the mantel over the fireplace chimed. He smelled of cigars and aftershave.

"Uncle John, what kind of business do you have downtown?" I asked. His wig was slightly off center, and I easily made out the seam above his ears.

"Mainly a manipulation of money," he said, lowering his paper. "All business comes to that one way or another. Nothing very complicated or ennobling about the endeavor."

"I thought you might be a banker," I lied.

"Never anything so grand. I did study law a year—just long enough to learn I wasn't cut out for a career before the bar."

I waited for more, but he raised the paper and continued reading. I worried that if I kept pestering him he'd become suspicious. That night at dinner he admired the daffodils my mother had cut in her garden and arranged in a red glass vase at the center of the table. He still wore the purple violet.

"The whole world seems to be blooming," he said.

"After such a cruel winter we deserve it," Aunt Rose May said. She'd become very soft toward him.

I wondered about the cuff links. I figured he must be selling them to a friend or maybe at the antique store or even a pawn shop, though I couldn't see Uncle John ever walking to gritty, besmirched Broad Street for that. He was too particular about his thin-soled, soft-leather shoes. The one thing he'd always done was polish them himself.

•   •   •

When Uncle John didn't come home Friday evening, I looked up and down Grove before bringing the paper in from the porch. Mama and Aunt Rose May held dinner and worked themselves into a dither. They couldn't find Uncle John's office number and pestered Information for it. They didn't know none existed.

At seven-twenty the blue-and-white Ford police cruiser stopped at the curb. The young officer took off his cap and wiped the sweat band as he talked to my mother. She lifted the fingers of both hands to her face. Uncle John had fallen through a barrier at the bridge excavation. The hospital needed instructions where to send the body.

He was buried beside Grandmother Harriet. None of the few remaining Rutledge cousins objected, despite their also owning a family plot. Mama cried and so did Aunt Rose May, though not as much. The fact they'd have to pay for the body's preparation, casket, hearse, and graveside service upset her. She never spoke those feelings outright, but she brittled up and rattled plates from the corner cupboard as if she meant to punish them.

Uncle John had a will naming Mama and Aunt Rose May the legatees, but left no property or money to distribute, not even a checking account. It was Aunt Rose May's idea to see a lawyer, Mr. Hawthorne Gaines at the firm of Polk, Hood, & Sydney. He believed the case valid, contending the contractor had been negligible in not protecting the public against risk of falling.

The construction company's attorney argued the excavation had been fenced with wire barriers, but somebody had removed a section. The insurance people settled out of court. Aunt Rose May wept the day the check came from Mr. Gaines.

"I miss him so," she said and sniffled as she eyed his place at the dinner table.

They discussed what they should do with his wigs and spats and puzzled over the empty slots in the walnut case. The last pair of cuff links, the everyday silver oval ones, had been buried with him.

I'd turned seventeen and kept thinking it had to be— Uncle John knew Aunt Rose May would go to a lawyer. It was her nature to be combative. On his birthday the September after his death, she and Mama were remembering him more than usual. My mother said she would've fixed him an angel food cake, and Aunt Rose May looked at the Spode tureen she no longer had the need to drop part of her pay in. Her green eyes wetted.

I finished eating dinner and left the house. I had a driver's license. I drove Mama's Buick over to Carytown where the high school crowd hung out. I got carded at Buck's Stop and paid a senior nicknamed Geek to buy me a cold six-pack.

I drank three beers fast. I might've made out with Lucy Whitmore, a blond John Marshall baton twirler, but didn't try. Back at the house, I hid the undrunk cans behind garden implements stacked in the garage.

I called goodnight to Mama and Aunt Rose May, who were watching Billy Graham on TV. I hurried up the steps before they could look me over and sniff me out. I lay on my bed, which started spinning every time I closed my eyes, and had this crazy idea. I stood, steadied myself by reaching to my dresser, and opened a drawer to feel around under my clean shirts. I tiptoed down the steps and snuck out the back.

Drinking a warm beer, I drove to Riverwood Cemetery. The grilled iron gate was locked. I climbed the stone wall and ran shining my flashlight on glaring tombstones and along black twisting paths that swallowed the beam.

I tripped over an oak tree's thick root and righted myself on a looming stone angel. A night breeze disturbed drooping willows and carried the scent of honeysuckle as well as the sharp odor of tobacco curing in warehouses across the river. I stumbled at Uncle John's plot, the soil not yet leveled like Grandmother Harriet's or my father's empty grave.

I lifted the bugle. I licked the mouthpiece, which tasted sour. My lip was loose because of beer and my not keeping up trumpet practice. Swaying, I tried twice before I got Taps halfway right. Still it sounded puny in the vast, cavernous world of tombs and night.

The guard ran hollering from darkness. He shone his flashlight right in my face. I shaded my eyes.

"What you doing, boy?" he asked, a hefty black wearing a uniform, cap, and badge. In his other hand he carried a wooden billy.

"Honoring two dead soldiers," I said and drew myself straight.

"Might be, but you hauling it out of this place quick as your feet'll roll you."

He gripped my arm and walked me to the gate, which he unlocked by using a key unhooked from his belt.

"What battle they die in?" he asked, releasing my arm, his voice quieter, more concerned. He opened the Buick's door for me.

"World wars," I said as I slid inside the car. I started the engine and switched on the headlights, which pushed out through blackness to patterned gray stones of the wall. I still gripped the bugle.

"Yeah, well, been a couple of them, and you come back daytime between eight and eight," the guard said and shut the door.

I backed the Buick to turn, steering one-handed, and peered along the road. I glimpsed the dark flowing sheen of the river.

"And take care now, hear?" the guard called after me.

HUMILITY

The thing about my niece Flower is you can never be certain she's speaking facts. Not she sets out to bend the truth. Rather, thoughts hatched in her brain need to make the passage to her tongue and out her mouth. During the journey those thoughts often run off track. She looks astonished as if hearing the spoken words the first time herself.

"They having the terriblest time," she said of the Randolphs. "Gloria threw a dish of smoked oysters and hit the picture of Grandfather Edgar."

"Hold it," I said. We sat on my porch swing, the view down over the valley where the Cherry River ran full from spring rains and glistened through wild grasses of abandoned pasture. "How you know?"

"They the only ones around here that eat oysters," Flower said.

"You saw Gloria pick the dish up, throw it, and hit the picture?"

"Tom carried it to Elkins to buy new glass."

"But did you see the dish of oysters break the glass?"

"You think oysters just pick up and fly?" Flower asked.

Could get nowhere with her, a thin little thing generally excited around men, especially Tom Randolph who was lots of man. He'd played football at West Virginia University, sold steel for Wheeling-Pittsburgh, and married Gloria, a girl from Philadelphia whose father manufactured drills, bits, boiler plate, and barbed wire. Tom, cousin to me twice removed through Grandfather Edgar, brought Gloria to Shawnee Valley.

The valley had known its day during timbering years when trees taller across the butt than Belgian drag horses standing head high were felled and floated down the river. There'd been boom towns, new banks, and painted ladies who beckoned loggers to yellow row houses.

Lumber barons built mansions, a few with tennis courts and swimming pools, and a Scotsman named Logan, who started as a pack paddler, transformed his acres into a golf course. Ravens cried over it, and foxes ran from bushes to attack rolling skipping balls, believing them wild tasty game.

Grandfather Edgar had lived in the largest mansion, it made of limestone blocks. He'd heaped his money not timbering or drumming dry goods but by operating a tannery. He'd also built the old Stonewall Jackson Hotel by the river, which burned during World War I and drove poker players out under the Indian cigar tree to finish their game of five card.

Tom'd been born in the mansion, yet the forests were skinned while he was still a boy, and like most of the population, his folks left Shawnee Valley, carrying him along.

It was a time of despair. The row houses wanted paint and became swaybacked, red oak roots broke up the roads, and bull thistles grew from the old Scotsman's golf course. Bear hunters ran hounds right through the village. Ivy climbed the mansion, boys threw Osage oranges at the window glass, and grackles nested in what had been a chandelier hanging above a table once set with fine china and polished silver.

But Tom grew to nurse a dream. He conjured boyhood memories of a sweet green land, a clear splashing river, the freshness of mountain mornings, shimmering brook trout twisting among cold ripples, elderberry blooms, and grouse drumming under hemlock shadows.

He was a big man, broad of face, and full of life. He'd walk out on the porch in his underwear shorts and just holler across the valley for the goodness of hearing his voice echoing back. He liked clowning around and painted yellow stripes on the back of every cat he could catch. While helping repaint the rusting ninety-five-foot-high water tank, he climbed to its crown, where he stood with his arms raised and gave the Tarzan call that in the movies brought elephants crashing through native villages.

Blond and fair, his wife, Gloria, had been to schools in New England and Europe. She was a golfer, skier, airplane pilot, and only child of a fiery-eyed, grizzled little man who had the manners of a gentleman and the business morals of a Gypsy horse trader. He could chew nails and spit tacks. His weakness was indulging her, and hers her love for Tom.

Tom had been worrying himself sick about what could be done to prevent Shawnee Valley from reverting altogether to a briar-tangled wilderness. Well Shawnee Valley had a mountain named Big Boy and the old golf course. For Gloria connecting the two was as natural as me baking bread.

First they fixed up the mansion—cleaned out rubble, the trash hoboes had left, the bird and rat droppings, the hunched coons that growled from rafters.

Tom hired carpenters, electricians, and plumbers from as far away as Buckhannon. New wells were dug, growed-up fields bushhogged, and lawns reseeded. A black maid from Philadelphia appeared, her name Viola, and she wore uniforms. Though Gloria owned two cars, she also needed horses. She couldn't seem to leave the house without riding in or on something.

"Surprised her feet hasn't withered off little as she uses them," Kenneth, my balding, belt-busting husband said. He'd worked most of his life for the B&O Railroad and night rose to listen to No. 5 highball along the river. The wind had to blow from the south in order to hear, but he'd sit up anyhow.

"I've smoked pipes, stogies, and cigarettes," he said. "Who'd smoke an oyster?"

Tom was busy buying land and laying out the ski slope. Designers and engineers who drove to Shawnee Valley rode our ridges in Jeeps. Tom wore laced high boots, whipcord britches, chamois shirts, and a campaign hat. He seemed always to be unrolling blueprints or bending to a transit.

"We'll build a lodge," he told people. "Tourists will flock here from the cities. There'll be jobs and wages for everybody. This land will bloom and have young people picking daisies."

We, the survivors, weren't so sure. We'd learned to make do. Kenneth had his pension, I quilted, and on days the welfare checks arrived at the post office you met folks from the hollows you'd believed were long gone or dead.

I went calling on Gloria. Not only distant kin to Tom, I was also sort of the village's unofficial first lady 'cause my daddy had been the last mayor of Shawnee Valley. I drove Kenneth's Ford pickup to the mansion late Saturday afternoon.

After sandblasting, the limestone shone like fresh cream on green velvet. Gloria had fancy friends visiting, all spirited and high style like her. The women wore high heels and bright colored tight slacks. Kenneth would've snorted. In Shawnee Valley the men had the saying, "Ridiculous as a woman in pants."

I'd dressed go-to-meeting in my blue print, white gloves, and straw hat with the chickadee. Her guests held glasses but stopped drinking to look at me.

"Call me Gloria," she said, which was a surprise because I never intended to do anything else. "Fix you a tod?"

She didn't really want me to stay. Her guests watched and waited. Likely they considered me hillbilly picturesque. From outsiders I was used to that.

I'd carried her a rhubarb cake. She handed it off to the maid Viola. I doubted Gloria or Viola either had ever tasted rhubarb. I'd picked it from the garden behind my house and taken a prize with the recipe at the Pocahontas County Fair.

"I don't have anything against good liquor, but I usually wait till the oak's shadow crosses my roses," I said, speaking of the ancient tree in my front yard. Kenneth could tell time to within ten minutes of the clock by that shadow.

"We're celebrating," she said, walking me to the door. "We finally received the last of our permits and are ready to let contracts."

Lord, Lord, the building activity, the disturbed dust, the sounds of saws, hammers, and machinery over the land. Deer stepped from woods and peered at workers.

Red-tailed hawks circled and screeched protests. Men hiked down from Big Boy Mountain and hunkered in hemlock shade to watch others labor—a free show.

Gloria was kindly, polite, and genteel in most ways, yet she had her father in her blood, that streak of mule and fire that caused him to stand up to the union and get himself hit on the head with a brick thrown during a strike.

When she rode her mare to where hired hands poured footings for the lodge, laid out fairways, and cleared a right-of-way for the ski lift, she couldn't keep from voicing her opinion any more than breathing. She came upon Wee Woolly Willie Ackers who sat with his back against a hickory tree eating a mutton sandwich not during the regular lunch break but ten-thirty in the morning.

"How many times a day do you feed yourself?" she asked.

" 'Bout six," Wee Woolly Willie said, not fooling. He weighed three hundred pounds, and his brown hair and bushy beard were so snarled no barber would risk shears on them. Wee Woolly Willie had never been accused of being smart, yet was strong, willing, and dependable in his way. You just had to allow him to do things at his own pace. He'd never harness to a team.

"You're not being paid to put on more fat," Gloria said, her chestnut mare pawing and prancing. Gloria wore black leather boots, yellow britches, and a yellow sleeveless shirt.

"Not getting paid for bitch bossing either," Wee Woolly Willie answered her.

"What'd you just say to me?" Gloria asked, her face aflame.

"Only horse I ever seen got two hind ends on it," Wee Woolly Willie said.

The men standing around leaning over shovels and

grubbing hoes believed she'd ride straight at Wee Woolly Willie and slash him with her crop, but he reared slow and high, and charging him would've been about as smart as attacking a black bear dipping into a honey tree. She wheeled the mare and galloped hell-bent up the slope to the mansion.

"Hillbilly trash," she called Wee Woolly Willie and demanded Tom fire him. That was a problem for Tom because Wee Woolly Willie had so much kin back through the hills and hollows that at election time the lieutenant governor made special trips to shake their hands and saw to it an underling passed out pint bottles of liquor from the trunk of the unmarked state car.

The law shied off during politicking, and some men stayed so drunk they couldn't remember how they'd got from October to December without noticing leaves had dropped from the trees.

Not only was Wee Woolly Willie richly kinned, men in our part of the country didn't care to work for women. They didn't like their women working either except around the house or milking and tending gardens.

Most our men after their fashion respected ladies, tipped their hats, and never cussed while a female was present, yet years of custom had drawn a line, and Gloria had stepped over it with Wee Woolly Willie.

What Tom had on his hands wasn't exactly a strike but rather a slowdown plus workers claiming to be sick, quitting early, or just not showing up. He'd leased lots of expensive construction equipment, and everything had to be on track for the first major snowfall of the season or lose the expected revenue from the skiing crowd.

He did his best to mend fences. He mixed with the men,

swung a brush axe himself, operated a bulldozer. During lunch breaks he'd settle among workers, joke with them, offer to share his sandwiches and thermos of ice water. The men liked and respected him, yet they wanted him to keep Gloria home and out the way.

Tom talked to her. Don't know whether Flower got all her facts right, likely not, but she told around what she heard from Viola.

Viola-through-Flower said Tom arrived home, showered the sweat and grime off himself, and joined Gloria's weekend guests who played croquet on the front lawn. Tom felt bone weary. The guests were drinking and changing the game, introducing all sorts of new rules, like you had to hit backwards between your legs or left-handed, one eye closed, and Tom, normally friendly and considerate, for once was out of humor and just set his mallet in the rack and walked in the house.

"I come home worn to a nub," he told Gloria, who followed. "My arms and legs are heavy as bagged cement, and you and your friends are looped and frolicking out there like it's party time."

"You think I don't work?" she asked. "Who sees the stalls are mucked out and the paddock fence painted? Who's picking out furniture and decor for the lodge? Who chooses the food set on the table and called Daddy to talk him into seeing our line of credit is extended at the bank?"

"You holding money over my head?" Tom asked. According to Viola-through-Flower, he sat on the front steps too tired to climb them.

"I'm telling you I hold up my end and need a little civilized recreation now and again," she said.

"Okay, sorry," he said, wiping his face. "We both been going at it too hard and under a strain. It's just work's falling behind. Like two steps backwards for every one forward."

"I'm sorry too," she said and sat by him on the steps. "I'll send Freddy and the others packing if you want."

"What I want and am requesting is for you to make it up with Wee Woolly Willie."

"Make it up? You mean apologize?"

"You don't need go right up to his face and eat crow. You could bake him a cake or tin of cookies."

"I don't bake cake and cookies for the help, especially when they're bearded, snaggled-toothed, and smell like skunk."

"Then please keep away from the men while they work, assuming I can get that to happen again."

"You're confining me to the house and grounds?" she asked and stood, hands on hips. "I won't be shut in."

Yet she tried to avoid causing trouble. She still rode out on her mare but circled construction sites and followed trails Tom had ordered cut for her among the hemlocks, red oaks, and shelly bark hickories. She tended to the flower garden and stood an easel on the mansion porch to paint a picture of Big Boy Mountain and the puffy white clouds drifting over it.

Tom politicked to bring more workers back on the job. He visited families, hunkered in milking sheds, and complimented the ladies on their hams, beaten biscuits, and sweet-potato pies. He talked about his childhood in the valley and how he'd coon hunted, lain on his belly to catch brook trout, and collected chinkapins to sell along the highway.

Gloria itched for action. She hummed with energy and had meant to be overseeing the interior completions of the lodge as well as the ski shop. She had plans for entertaining paying guests—spelunking, wildflower hikes, fishing and raft trips down the Cherry River.

"It's a case of exploiting what's already here," she told those who'd listen. "And spreading the word. When this valley becomes known in the right places, we'll need walls to keep people out."

But then, according to Viola-through-Flower, the matter of Gloria wearing shorts down to the village came up.

"I just stopped to buy gasoline," she said.

"You stepped from the car."

"If I can't step from my car on my own land, this country can go to hell."

The Gulf station belonged to the Shawnee Valley Corporation but was operated by Wayne "Rapid" Ripley. He held title to being the slowest-moving man in the valley and seemed to be retreating even walking forward.

"Not with long bare legs like yours while Bible Study's letting out," Tom said.

"Screw Bible Study," Gloria said, words overheard by Viola and passed on to Flower, who was shocked.

"But me, I love your legs," Tom said. He hugged, kissed, and cooled her heat.

At the first snow, Tom and Gloria climbed the ski run for a tryout. They left curved tracks along the slope. They celebrated, Viola claimed, with dancing, champagne, and other frolicking.

Gloria offered to teach the valley children how to ski. She was disappointed and hurt only a few showed up, though she supplied paraphernalia free.

"Do their mothers think I'm a loose woman?" she asked Tom.

"They resent men's eyeballs hanging to their knees every time you pass wearing stretch pants and tight sweaters."

"I'll not be a hag and you know what? I think I'll just take time out and visit my daddy down in Boca. Keep your hands off me. I'm not changing my mind."

"I need you here and when you coming back?"

"When I feel warm, toasted, and like a sea creature."

Viola with her, Gloria drove off so fast she skidded her red foreign car into the ditch. She rassled it back up to the road, honked her horn, and sped away. Rapid Ripley, who was using his tractor and blade to scrape aside a snow drift, claims she lifted a finger at him in the manner men sometimes do.

She stayed gone a month and returned tanned, her hair bleached, Viola again beside her. She found workers swarming about the lodge and the second leg of lift pylons set in concrete up the mountain.

Tom had been caring for her mare as well as doing his own cooking, though I invited him down to my house once a week for Sunday dinner. He was wild to see Gloria, she him. They clamped onto each other, hurried up to the mansion, and didn't show till morning. Viola-through-Flower claimed there was laughter, shrieks, and what sounded like footraces on the second floor.

Early spring Gloria came to visit me, only the second time she'd been to my house. Kenneth had gone fishing, and I'd just planted radishes in my garden. They, English peas, Irish 'taters, and leaf lettuce were the first things I put in the ground each season.

She didn't wear britches or ski sweaters but a proper dove-gray dress and hose. She kept her skirt pushed over her knees as we swung on my porch. She admired my budding rosebushes. She looked lovely, tan of her face like fine silk setting off her pretty teeth.

"It's happening," she said, smiling and motioning toward Big Boy Mountain and sounds of construction. "Tom's so happy and proud. His dream come true. Aunt Dittie, I don't want to go wrong again. I've come for help. Tell me how to make my peace in the valley."

"Attend church and Bible Study," I said. "Join our quilting circle. Take people cakes and pies. Cut down on perfume and eye paint. Let Tom do most the talking. Start a baby."

She stared at me from eyes the color of purple gentians. Her lips trembled, and her slim fingers gripped themselves.

"My, you certainly have answers. What you prescribe might be a bit difficult for a modern gal who plays scratch golf, foxhunts, and has flown a P-51. All right, I won't do anything out of the ordinary without first consulting you, though I don't know whether I can manage a baby by the time the lodge opens. Last I heard it still requires nine months."

"If you show, it's the same thing."

She looked at her stomach and stroked it like a pet cat.

"You poor thing, you'd never be the same again," she told it.

I don't know anything about her and Tom making babies, yet she did try most of what I advised her. She attended church, the regular service, Bible Study, Christian Endeavor, and Wednesday night Prayer Meeting.

Reverend Amos Arbogast at the Cool Spring Baptist was

so pleased he nigh wore out his backbone bobbing before
her. She dropped generous contributions into the offering
basket and didn't have a bad singing voice either. She drew
the line, however, at allowing him to duck her in a Cherry
River baptism.

She sewed with us women, despite she knew about as
much about quilting as a cow did about flying. She sat
around the big oak table in the cinderblock Community
House and listened to us women talk canning, hog killing,
and the best way to cure colic, which the general opinion
held was a teaspoonful of damson preserves mixed with
honey and a thimble of corn liquor.

Her Jeep had a flat, and she acted as if she didn't understand how to change a tire but called for Rapid Ripley to
fix it. She smiled up at him so nice and helpless he removed
his cap.

She quieted around Tom too, held her tongue when he
talked among the men, hung back patiently till he was
ready to leave. You'd have thought he was giving her the
grandest gift in the world by just allowing her to stand at
his side.

Everything went fine till tonic time. In Shawnee Valley
we gathered ramps, tasty little wild scallions plentiful on
the mountainside. The old folks, which included me, believed nothing cleaned out the system like ramps, not even
Black Draught. Ramps is nature's way of providing a body
flush.

Yearly each spring the men climbed Big Boy Mountain
collecting them. We ladies cooked them up in everything
from scrambled eggs and sausage to baked bread and
puddings.

There's a hitch. Ramps lay an odor on your breath and

through your pores near as bad as a henhouse during dog days. People won't approach within ten feet of you even upwind if you've eaten them and they haven't. Shawnee Valley's answer is everybody does eat ramps, and low and behold they cancel out your smell and you theirs.

Why the village hounds slink away from rampers, but after forty-eight hours of nature's helper working, if you could just slip out your intestines and sight them at the sky, they'd appear as clean and shiny as a freshly oiled rifle barrel.

Gloria knew nothing about ramps. Tom'd asked me for my specialty, a ramp cabbage casserole. At his urging, Gloria was reluctant to try it but finally did and loved it. Viola too.

"Has a unique flavor," Gloria said. "Never tasted anything quite like it. Truly exotic."

Gloria would've been all right had not some of her Philadelphia friends stopped by on their way to White Sulphur and the Greenbrier. They asked about the mansion's peculiar odor and wouldn't stay for dinner. Gloria blew steam.

"They turned their faces aside and stepped back from me," she said. "I've never been more embarrassed. I've always been proud of my hygiene. They acted as if they smelled Wee Woolly Willie. You and your jokes. You talked me into eating that damned mess."

And during her fit she threw the dish of smoked oysters hurriedly prepared for the unexpected company, and it struck Grandfather Edgar's picture.

She also packed, threw things in her red car, and left the village with Viola. Took Gloria's dust fifteen minutes to settle. Tom stood on the lawn looking after her. He kicked the mounting block so hard he limped lopsided back into the mansion.

Flower smiled.

Tom at last got the lodge, golf course, and ski lift finished. Workers tried a new machine, and for a few minutes we had snow in late August. He mailed out pretty colored brochures that described Shawnee Valley as "a complete mountainside adventure."

He came to see me Saturday afternoon while I pulled the last of my butterbeans. Fattening rain clouds formed above the river. We'd have a shower sure enough. Down by the river cattle whisked their tails in shade of the birches. Up the mountain, windows of the new lodge reflected sunlight, and the glass glittered with the bluish tint of dragonfly eyes.

"What made her maddest was her old boyfriend Freddy Cadwallader was there," Tom said, his gray town suit needing the feel of an iron, his black socks drooping, his shoes unshined. "Old Freddy drew off from kissing her. Then the others edged away. She believes they now all think she has body odor. I don't know what to do."

"Where is she?" I asked.

"Golfing. All over Hell's half acre. Gone crazy for the game."

"Let me study a spell," I said.

When he left, I set on my thinking cap. I thought hard during supper, after prayers, and first thing in the morning. No way around I had to put my feet on the path. I stopped Tom driving his Jeep through the village.

"Let me know when next you wind her," I said.

"Don't think she'd care for that expression," he said.

Later during the week he learned she was at Williamsburg, Virginia, for the Women's Tidewater Amateur. Friday morning I dressed before daybreak, fed the chickens, and made Kenneth ride me to Elkins where I bought a Greyhound ticket.

"This costing money," Kenneth said.

"We're not poorhouse yet," I said.

"What'll you do if you find her?"

"Keep my own counsel," I said.

"Don't I know," he said.

I changed buses in Staunton and Richmond before reaching Williamsburg. I asked a taxi driver how much to carry me to the Old Dominion Country Club. He said eighteen dollars. I told him I'd walk.

"You can't walk seven miles," he said. He had a tattoo on the upper muscle of his right arm—a hula dancer who wiggled when he flexed his wrist.

"Do it before breakfast ever' morning," I said, which was almost the truth if you counted chores.

"Get in, lady. I'll drive you for ten."

"Five," I said, opening my pocketbook.

"Jesus," he said.

"Glad to know our Savior's name is known to your tongue," I said.

He drove me to a brick gateway that had stone pineapples on top the posts. A guard wearing dark sunglasses told me to buy a ticket. I told him I needed to speak to Gloria Randolph.

"She can't speak, she's playing," he said.

"Want to bust up a marriage?" I asked.

"Stop a tornado easier than her," the taxi driver said.

The guard readjusted those sunglasses to look me over. I

don't guess I appeared high style. While I might buy myself a scarf or pair of shoes, mostly I had made my clothes, including the straw hat with the chickadee on top.

"Wait," he said and walked off to speak to a man wearing a blue blazer and white trousers. Pinned to a lapel was a tag that read Official. He introduced himself as Henry W. Willard and asked was it an emergency. I answered yes. He would, he said, ride me in his cart parked beside the gate.

"How much you charging?" I asked.

"Courtesy of the management," he said and smiled, not a bad-looking fellow, though his white hair had growed thin and he smelled of lilac aftershave.

He drove me over grass greener than creek moss, down around a pond, and toward a crowd. I held to my hat. We stopped at a rope barrier. Mr. Willard spoke into a walkie-talkie he pulled from a leather holster attached to the cart.

"She's on fourteen," he said to me.

We left the cart and walked a sandy, pine-strewn path. I spotted Gloria through a gap of spectators. She wore checkered shorts, a white sleeveless shirt, and a long-billed yellow cap. Her pretty tan legs were bare high up. She and three other ladies held golf clubs. One bent low over a ball. She popped it into the hole, it thunked, and people clapped.

Gloria's turn. She knelt to squint at her ball and the hole. She circled them. They could've been timber rattlers.

"An important putt," Mr. Willard whispered. "She'll move into third if she drops this ball."

"Why'd she drop it when it's already on the ground?" I asked, and he looked at me funny.

Gloria stepped to the ball and set her feet. She glanced at the crowd, frowning and waiting for yappers to quiet.

Maybe it was my chickadee that caught her eye. She blinked, straightened, and crossed toward me.

"Aunt Dittie, that you?" she called.

"Let's go home," I said.

"Can't you see what I'm doing?" she asked. People watched, including men toting and aiming cameras.

"What I see is you chasing a little ball when your loving husband waits home not eating properly and needs the loving arms of a dutiful wife."

"Resume play," another blue-blazered, tagged official told Gloria.

"It's not play for Tom," I said. "He's losing weight and looks like he's been run over by a herd of cattle."

"Can't talk now," Gloria said, her face flushed, her eyes cutting around. She started off.

"You'll not find a better man in a million years," I spoke after her, and cameras swung to me.

"You'll have to hush," Mr. Willard said, touching my shoulder.

"You believe it's more important to knock a little white ball around than saving a marriage?" I asked him and the crowd. "It's pure foolishness is what it is. Whether she gets that ball in the hole won't make a dime's worth of difference a couple of days from now. It's a God-awful shame. Marriage is a blessed sacrament and binding oath. Thousand times more important than whacking balls into holes."

People stared, cameras clicked, somebody tittered. Gloria dropped her putter, covered her face, and ran toward the plantation clubhouse bordering a lake that reflected white clouds.

Mr. Willard carried me in his electric cart after her. I

thanked him for the ride. He shook his head and smiled. Not a bad-looking man at all.

I found Gloria boohooing in the ladies locker room. She looked a mess, but a pretty one. Break any man's heart and most women's. She poked fingers at tears.

"I might've won," she cried and sniffled into a towel. "I've never been closer."

"Don't be silly. Your promise before God is not words you can take back and besides aren't you weary of lying in the bed without your man? Tom's growing puny. Looks like he's been chewed on by rats. Needs help at the lodge now guests'll be arriving. Needs you."

"Let him ask me," she said and buried her face in the towel.

"He sent me to do that."

"Makes him a coward."

"But a loving coward. Men made in all shapes and sizes. None come perfect. Now I'm hungry, worn to the bone, and want to go home. Give me a ride?"

She sobbed, bucked, blew her nose, and sighed. "I'll shower first," she said.

We drove back during the night. She stopped at Hardee's for me to eat an egg biscuit. The sun broke over the spruce pines on Big Boy Mountain just as we rode into Shawnee Valley. The September morning broke fresh, a milky mist causing hemlocks to drip and grass to glisten.

"Far as I go," she said at my house and climbed out. "If he wants me, let him come begging."

I ambled up to see Tom. I told him to walk small—which he did later by hiking down to the village, a cow bell in one hand, a police whistle in the other. He rang the bell, blew the whistle, and shouted, "Hear ye, hear ye, I love my wife and would swim the seven seas for her."

He stripped down to his polka-dot undershorts and swam to the other side of the Cherry River and back. His khakis again pulled on, his wet black hair stringing down his face, he moved along ringing the bell, blowing the whistle, and calling, "Woe, woe is me."

All the racket drew a gaping crowd. Children followed him, and the village dogs circled and barked.

"I'd walk on my knees for my bride," he shouted and crossed the road on those knees to my front yard. He snatched up grass and scattered it over his head. "Forgive this poor miserable sinner."

Gloria peeked from a window. Still kneeling, Tom picked a red rose off my Elizabethan Beauty bush and stuck the bloom in his mouth. As he chewed, Gloria sidled onto my porch. Hands behind her back, she'd already begun to giggle.

"Tasty it is, yet nothing like the lips of my beloved," Tom hollered. He rolled his eyes upward and tossed aside the whistle and cowbell. He abjectly spread his palms. "Your slave, ma'am."

"You fool," she said, hurried to him, and tugged him by his wet hair to kiss his mouth. Laughing, they spit out red petals. They smooched, pinched, and jabbed each other. As they walked holding each other around the waist down the road, Tom got hiccups, and Gloria slapped his back. The circling dogs yapped at them. I figured baby making had to be on the menu.

"Isn't it beautiful?" Flower asked, weeping into her pink hanky, she both happy and sad, knowing Tom lost for good this time, though she never had a hair of him in the first place.

"Damn if I thought a woman could make any man to crawl on his belly like that," my husband Kenneth said. He and a bunch of other men in the village were disgusted.

"Just you be careful how you talk to me," I told him.

STONES

The liver-and-white pointers, Zack and Rattler, ranged wide across lespedeza that rasped Chip's leather-faced hunting britches. His father still allowed him only eight shells—that number the bobwhite limit in Virginia. Chip had to account for each fired, and if he averaged more than two per bird, his father acted as if he'd bitten into an unripe persimmon.

The father's counting of shells had been part of Chip's training to make him bring the walnut stock to his cheek and level his eyes along the entire length of the L. C. Smith's sixteen-gauge side-by-side. He frequently carried home meat on a bird-for-shell average, pleasing his father who kidded him by asking, "You ain't shooting them on the ground?"

This day was November 20, the opening shoot of the new season, and the dogs dropped on point midway across the field. Before Chip reached them, he saw the new fence—three strands of barbed wire stapled to freshly cut cedar posts. Red soil had been tamped around the base of each post, and on every other one a No Trespassing sign had been tacked.

Zack and Rattler were stanch. Their tails spiked upward, and the partridge scent was so strong their bodies trembled.

Chip, the L. C. Smith held high, stepped forward between them.

The covey erupted right at the fence line and swung left. He dropped a bird that flew high and then a sleeper. He watched the covey glide down among sunlit pines edging the field. The two birds had fallen on the other side of the fence. The dogs waited for his command to fetch. He sent them across with the underhanded motion of pitching a softball.

Zack found the sleeper. He retrieved it, his mouth working feathers, but his teeth never punctured flesh. Chip took it from him, smoothed the feathers of the cock bird wetted by Zack's saliva, and stuck it in the game pouch of his canvas vest. He'd already drawn two more No. 8s from loops of the vest and thumbed them into the shotgun's chambers.

Rattler hadn't located the second bird. Zack joined in to work the lespedeza. The bobwhite had been winged and was running. Chip stood at the fence. He read the name written at the bottom of the posted sign: A. I. Benjamin.

Still the dogs didn't find the bird. He looked toward the house. This property was called the Gatlin Place. Once it'd been a three-thousand-acre plantation mostly given to the growing of dark-fired tobacco. Julius Temple Gatlin, the patriarch whose portrait hung in the courthouse, had raised a troop to ride with Jeb Stuart and died a judge at ninety-six while sitting on the bench trying a horse-thieving case.

Over the years portions had been sold off or leased out by Gatlin women. Georgia Pacific had bought a section for saw timber that ran all the way down to the Hidden River.

The house had been abandoned. Wisteria and briars rioted in the family graveyard and box bushes of a formal garden.

The dogs again jerked on point. Chip'd never be able to whistle or order them off a stand. He could fire the L. C. Smith, which might cause them to break, yet the bird would most likely be left dead. He felt anger that anybody had fenced in a section of his prime hunting territory.

He pushed down the middle strand of barbed wire and ducked through. The dogs waited heads lowered, their eyes bugged at a honeysuckle patch. Chip stepped in boldly. He kicked his boot through honeysuckle. Still no bird. "Hie on!" he commanded.

Rattler bolted forward and came up with the partridge. It'd been hit by a single pellet through the breast and able to run a distance before dying. Chip allowed the dogs to mouth it, the reward for good work. He made over them, and as he fitted the bird in his game pouch, he heard the shout.

Hurrying across the field from the direction of the house came a man wearing a dark unbuttoned overcoat. Closer, Chip saw he was black. He had on a gray suit, vest, and black city shoes not meant for the scratch of lespedeza. Beggar lice stuck to his pants legs and the bottom of the overcoat.

"What's your name?" he demanded. He was stout, yet not soft. He had a round, pitted face. He wore gloves, not the work kind, but brown stitched leather.

"John Kincaid," Chip said. "I shot the birds on the other side of the fence and couldn't just leave them."

"Give them to me," the man said. His eyes were so dark they seemed to lack pupils.

"They didn't come from this side," Chip said.

"You picked them up off my land. Give them back to me or we discuss it with the game warden."

Discussing it with the game warden didn't sound like Howell County talk. Chip knew the General District Court judge, a hunter himself who taught Sunday School at the Olive Branch Methodist Church and was likely to be understanding of a trespass case. When the man held out a gloved hand, Chip hesitated, then drew the birds from his pouch and tossed them on the ground.

"That's where they come from on your side of the fence," he said. As he bowed back through the barbed wire, something struck his back. The nigger had thrown the birds at him.

"Mister, you're pretty dumb doing that to a man holding a gun," Chip said.

" 'Man' you call yourself?" he asked and laughed. "One razor blade would've lasted you your lifetime up to now. Don't cross my line ever again."

For an instant Chip felt hot and the shotgun wanting to lift. At least fan the nigger and send him running in his city clothes. But that could bring jail time, the loss of freedom. He eased his thumb off the safety and spat before whistling in the dogs. When he looked back, the nigger had picked up the birds and was carrying them toward the house.

He didn't tell his father everything. His daddy was a switchman for Norfolk Southern and had a temper. He broke dogs hard, laying onto them with a leather strap he carried hooked to his belt if they failed to honor points or chewed a bird. At the dinner table Chip did mention the fence.

His mother heard something in his voice. When the

father went to the weekly Tuesday fire meeting, she asked what'd happened.

"Just let it alone," she said after Chip finished telling all. She was a small, wiry woman who worked at the shoe factory. "You got plenty of other hunting territory."

The father found out about Mr. A. I. Benjamin by asking around at the firehouse. Abram Isaac Benjamin had bought the house through a Lynchburg real estate agent. Benjamin was from New York, and that was enough to blacken him in Howell County no matter the color of his skin.

"What's he fixing to do with the Gatlin Place?" the old men and ne'er-do-wells loafing around Tobaccoton's courthouse elm asked. Rumor was he meant to cut off and sell lots. What'd happen to land values if he brought down a bunch of uppity niggers? Maybe they'd be a heathen religious cult that wore sheets and turbans.

Despite what Chip's mother told him, he sure didn't mean to allow Mr. A. I. Benjamin to keep him off that part of the land on the near side of the fence. He wouldn't shoot birds across it but take all he could get right up to the line.

During January, the last week of the season, he drove his Dad's '77 rattling longbody Ford pickup out to the tract. The weather was warm and windy, not good for scenting. Worn down to rib-showing lean, Zack and Rattler went about finding birds in trifling fashion.

As Chip directed them along the fence line, he heard a cry on the wind. If a cry. He listened thinking maybe the sound had been caused by a white-oak tree limb scraping against roof tin of a broken Gatlin outbuilding.

There it was again, surely a voice. He drew the shells from his gun before crossing through the barbed wire. He ordered the dogs to heel and walked toward the house—a sprawling frame dwelling with four brick chimneys and verandas upstairs and down.

A building permit had been nailed to a scabby white oak. The Gatlin place must've once been grand, but wind and weather had peeled off the paint, slates were missing from the roof, and the empty windows stared out like outraged eyes.

Chip climbed the rickety steps to the front porch and shouted a hello through the sagging open door.

"Up here," the voice answered.

Chip entered the front hall. Plaster had fallen. There was a large hole in the ceiling where a light or chandelier must've hung. Broken bottles lay on the floor, and mantels had been torn from the fireplaces. Moldy hay bales were stacked in what'd once been a dining room or parlor.

He looked up the curved staircase. The window on the landing was gone. He commanded the dogs to stay before starting to climb. The steps felt shaky. Soles of his boots crunched glass. On the second floor he looked down a hallway. The floor was covered by chunks of plaster, and dirt daubers had built nests on exposed lathing. All light fixtures had been ripped out, and twisted wires dangled.

"Hurry," the voice called.

He looked into what had likely been a bedroom. Strips of stained, faded wallpaper curled down to the baseboards. Mr. A. I. Benjamin lay among a pile of bricks. Part of a chimney had fallen in on him. The dry mortar had floured him and his bib overalls white.

"Can't move my leg," he said and clenched his eyes.

Chip started to tell him too damn bad, go to hell, and might've left, but thought of his mother. She was chairlady of the Women of the Church down at Olive Branch Methodist. She would never turn her back on suffering. He felt she was watching him. He leaned his L. C. Smith against the door frame, tested the floor as he moved forward, and checked the gap in the chimney to be sure no more of it was about to come down.

He lifted bricks off Mr. A. I Benjamin, who sweated and bit back pain. When Chip got him uncovered, Mr. A. I. Benjamin's right leg bent funny. He dragged himself across the floor and puked.

"You drive me to a doctor?" he whispered. He was hunched and panting.

"I never yet left a gutshot deer in the woods," Chip said and helped him stand. Benjamin cried out in pain as he rose and leaned his stinking weight on Chip. As they worked down the steps, grains of plaster sprinkled them. Mr. A. I. Benjamin tried to swallow his hurtings, but they forced groans. He was near to weeping.

His car, a black Mercedes, was parked behind the house. It was a clean, recent model, a SEL 420, and one of a kind in Howell County. Even the doctors, lawyers, and bankers drove only Caddys and Lincolns.

"Just help me lie across the backseat," Mr. A. I. Benjamin said, sweat lodged in pits of his twisted face.

"Going to mess up your car," Chip said. "Need to take my dogs part way too."

"Do it."

Chip resented being ordered about but had never before driven a Mercedes. Might never again. He whistled Zack and Rattler up front beside him on wine-colored seats that creaked like fine saddle leather. He stopped at the pickup and fastened the dogs in the box pen he and his daddy built to carry on the truck's bed during hunting season.

Benjamin fainted as they bumped out the rutted road. Chip left him at the Tobaccoton's Howell County Emergency Squad. Members lifted him onto a wheeled litter and would drive him to the Prince Edward County Community Hospital. Revived, Benjamin struggled to get his wallet in hand and tried to pay Chip a twenty-dollar bill.

Chip walked off without taking it, left the keys to the locked Mercedes with the squad, and hitched a ride on a billet truck to the pickup, all the while thinking an afternoon's hunt shot to hell.

When he got home from school Tuesday, his mother had set a letter for him between the salt and pepper shakers on the kitchen table. It was handwritten, the script printed: "James Lee Kincaid, Jr., has permission to hunt on all my property wheresoever situated." It was signed, "A. I. Benjamin."

After school let out in early June, Chip searched for a job. He usually measured tobacco for the Department of Agriculture, but Henry Boggs, a college boy, beat him to it. Like with everything, the choice involved politics. Henry's father was cousin to Lawrence Sutton, the Commonwealth's Attorney.

"I'll never vote for that sonofabitch again," Chip's father said and threw a clod of plowed garden dirt at the mother's calico cat. All bird hunters hated cats.

Chip stopped by Southside Hardware & Appliance hoping to get hired on as a clerk. Mr. A. I. Benjamin was in the store and must've overheard him talking to Gates

Hamlett, the owner. Mr. Asshole Idiot Benjamin waited outside the store. He again wore a gray suit and vest. The Mercedes was parked at the curb. He limped.

"You want work?" he asked.

"Not from you," Chip said and started away.

"You won't take six dollars an hour from a nigger?" Mr. A. I. Benjamin asked.

Six dollars an hour was two dollars and sixty-five cents above minimum wage. Chip craved a red '84 TransAm, a one-owner, low-mileage model he could get for two-hundred down and twenty-four monthly payments.

"For doing what?" he asked.

"I assume you can use a hammer and saw," Mr. A. I. Benjamin said.

Chip didn't like him any more than on that first day at the fence. Benjamin talked fancy, and the corners of his mouth turned down. Chip could use a hammer and saw. What country boy couldn't? He'd almost saved the down payment for the TransAm, and six dollars an hour steady work might keep him in wheels. What he didn't have was the prospect of a job anywhere else. And every day he feared the TransAm would sell off the lot down at Dixie Auto.

He drove the pickup to the Gatlin Place at nine o'clock Monday morning. Benjamin had cleared the wild growth around the house. He worked tearing slate off the roof. He'd parked his Mercedes alongside a cabin in the rear that most likely had once been a kitchen. Mortar crumbled and bled from between the bricks. Chip climbed a teetering aluminum ladder leaned to the eaves of the house.

"Be here by eight," Benjamin said. He wore the bib overalls as well as a straw hat and high-top clodhoppers.

"Get more done while it's cooler. Help yourself to the wrecking bar."

Chip pried and busted slate from the roof. The day turned hot. He stripped off his shirt and looked down along the wild greening fields he'd hunted. He thought of shots he'd made.

Out west of the house was the Gatlin cemetery surrounded by an iron fence that had tangles of honeysuckle and cow vine growing among the pickets. Elderly ladies of the clan who lived distant from Howell County had used to send servants to keep the cemetery mowed and weeded, but Gatlin blood had thinned, the line mostly bred out.

Chip worked without a break, at first extra careful of the roof, but the oak trusses felt solid, no give. Most slates were unbroken. He wondered why Benjamin meant to take them all off when a patching job might do.

"You need to put on another roof?" he asked.

"This one's served its time," Benjamin said without turning.

They both dripped sweat and slapped stinging greenies. Benjamin laid planks across exposed trusses to stand on. Slates thrown to the yard shattered.

"Could use a drink of water," Chip said, wiping sweat.

"You going to last even a day?" Benjamin asked, and this time pivoted to look at Chip out of those dark pupilless eyes. "There's a dipper at the well."

Chip climbed down the ladder. The well pump behind the house had been newly oiled, and the tin dipper hung from a wire hook. When he pushed and lifted the iron handle half a dozen times, water bubbled up cool. He didn't use the dipper. Instead he got a good flow going and cupped his palms under the stream. As he rose to swallow, he saw Benjamin watching from the roof.

Chip climbed back, and they worked without talking. Benjamin didn't seem to need water. Maybe he didn't mean to stop for lunch either, but he finally laid down his wrecking bar.

"You bring food?" he asked.

"I got me a baloney sandwich and a Sundrop," Chip said.

"Should've guessed," Benjamin said.

They climbed down the ladder. Benjamin limped to the well and as he drank looked over the dipper at Chip. He rinsed it before crossing to the old kitchen.

Chip sat on the pickup's tailgate to eat his sandwich. He'd parked in the shade of a hackberry and listened to a hawk's cry and the fuss it caused among crows in the pine woods. They chased after the hawk, dived at him, but that redtail flew on like crows weren't worth bothering about.

He'd hardly swallowed the last bite of his sandwich before Benjamin was again up the ladder to the roof. Not fifteen minutes had gone by. Chip thought of just getting in the damn pickup and driving off. He didn't want to be working for any kind of prick in the first place and especially a fancy New York nigger one.

But Benjamin owed him wages for what he'd already done, and Chip pictured the TransAm glittering on the lot down at Dixie Auto. He climbed the ladder. He went at it hard using the wrecking bar. He'd not ask again for water. He'd show what a country boy could do.

The sun reflected hot off slates. It fuzzed his eyes. His hands became slippery on the bar, though he was in shape.

He played guard for the Howell County High Rebels, yet felt himself giving out. He kept glancing at the sun to calculate quitting time.

The heat caused the air to shimmy and locusts to tune up, their screeching throbbing across the steamy fields. Because the wrecking bar was so slick in his fingers, he almost banged his foot. Flies sucked blood from his bare back. It had to be past five, and they hadn't finished the roof, but it was sure God time to give up work for the day.

Still Benjamin didn't quit. Chip felt dizzy as he looked at the ground. He steadied himself by reaching to a chimney. He started to say he had a date and needed to leave. Yet that meant the black bastard'd whipped him.

They bared the roof to the trusses, leaving just the platform of planks to stand on. Benjamin indicated Chip was to go first down the ladder. Chip threw the wrecking bar to the yard, and it cracked slate. He'd just about given out of strength.

Benjamin unbuttoned a bib pocket of his overalls and drew out his pocket watch. He crossed to the old kitchen. When he came back, he held six new ten-dollar bills.

"Take my money this time?" he asked.

Chip told himself he'd be goddamn if he'd work for Benjamin again, but throughout the night he kept seeing that TransAm scratching out to the blue yonder. He drove to the Gatlin Place the next morning at eight. Benjamin swung a sledge against a chimney. He pulled out his gold pocket watch to check whether Chip was late.

He put Chip to work removing trusses, which some carpenter during olden times had numbered in sequence using deeply chiseled Roman numerals. Why was Benjamin taking the trusses out? They were so sound Chip grunted like a hog to saw and lift them free.

"Don't you want to save them?" he asked.

"Just drop them right into the house," Benjamin said.

At lunch Chip again walked out to eat on the pickup's tailgate. Benjamin limped from the house and sat with his back against the hackberry. He pushed up the brim of his straw hat. He held a sandwich made of white bread and slab of rat cheese.

"Those trusses look all right to me," Chip said. "You could use 'em again."

"You a contractor?" Benjamin asked, his chewing steady.

"No," Chip said. "Are you?"

"I'm employed by a firm named Lilly," Benjamin said.

"You mean like Easter lilies and stuff?"

"No, Eli Lilly, but yes we peddle genetic flowers that in their design and bloom are marvels of intricate beauty. You know about genetics?"

"Something about genes?"

"You are correct," Benjamin said and laughed so hard he coughed and hocked up an oyster of ugly dark stuff. "Something about genes."

"Then what you doing here rebuilding a house?"

"I'm on sabbatical. And I enjoy working with my hands."

Chip didn't ask what a sabbatical was, and that afternoon they tore out the last trusses. They also sledged a chimney to the second floor level. Again Benjamin paid Chip with new bills for his time.

The rest of the week they worked at prizing loose the house's pine siding. A few boards had dried and warped, but most could be used after hammering out nails. Benjamin told him to throw them all, good or bad, on top the trusses.

When Chip got a drink at the pump, he saw the foot end of a cot in the old kitchen and that Benjamin had strung up a clothes line behind it. Benjamin had to be cooking too because he stayed away from town except to buy groceries and spoke never a word more than necessary to anybody. The gleaming Mercedes looked weirdly out of place parked beside the swayback building with its rusted roof and scaling mortar.

Friday after work Chip hurried to Tobaccoton and put the first payment down on the TransAm. Oh, she was sweet wheels, and the engine sang his song. He picked up Alice Anne, who had ash-blond hair and was a cheerleader at Lee-Jackson. They ate corn dogs at the Tastee Freez before going to the drive-in movie early so everbody'd see them in the car.

Buster Wesley didn't like Chip being with Alice Anne. He drove a '87 Thunderbird and pulled up alongside to ask how Chip liked rolling on nigger wheels. Chip hit him through the window, and they punched each other around till they got thrown out.

"I've a mind to make you take that car back," Chip's mother said when she saw his torn soiled clothes and bruised face. He'd tried to sneak in the house and keep them hidden.

"Boys got to fight over girls," his daddy said. "It's in the blood, and he whipped Buster."

"I'd like to whip the both of you," she said and banged a pan in the sink.

Sunday afternoon Chip took Alice Anne down to

Hidden River, and they fished off the bank. As they drove back at dusk with a mess of blue cats in a pail, he wondered what Benjamin did with himself of an evening. He drove in slow along the cedar-darkened lane to the Gatlin Place. Alice Anne saw Benjamin first. He was walking in the field east of the house, stopping, and jabbing a long pole or pipe into the ground.

"Fetching salad?" Alice Anne asked. She'd knotted her denim shirttails around sun pinked skin of her waist.

"Salad's all seeded up in this heat," Chip said.

They watched. Benjamin moved in a pattern by taking two steps, pausing, and jabbing the pole or pipe before moving on. As darkness settled, they saw only the white of his shirt.

"I got it," Chip said. "He's searching for oil."

"It's spooky," she said. "Let's hightail it out of here."

When Chip arrived at work Monday, Benjamin had finished knocking down a second chimney and started another. He lowered the eight-pound sledge and wiped sweat, which he flung aside. He gleamed like a greased skillet.

"Mule kick you?" he asked, breathing hard.

"Hardly a mule left in the county," Chip said. "Everything's tractor now."

"Didn't realize tractors had fists," Benjamin said.

He put Chip to work ripping down the second-story framing. Clothes hung on the line at the old kitchen. A black kettle sat on bricks of a makeshift fireplace. From the kettle stuck a lathing slat used for stirring. Chip first figured Benjamin must've been cooking himself a stew. Or boiling his clothes to wash them the way darkies used to do.

When they knocked off for lunch, Benjamin dug a

plastic fork into a can of Vienna sausage and produced apples for himself and Chip. Among tangles of wisteria Benjamin had found a stunted tree. The apples were shrunken, hard, and bitter. Chip took just one bite, but Benjamin finished his.

"Imagine a tree still bearing any kind of fruit on the soured soil of this place," Benjamin said.

Chip looked out toward the west where blackening rain clouds formed up. He'd been thinking about all the work they'd done. Benjamin stood from the hackberry.

"If I didn't know better, I'd say you wasn't rebuilding the house but tearing it down," Chip said.

"You're real smart for a redneck boy got kicked by a mule," Benjamin said.

"Why not just burn it?" Chip asked. "Save lots of effort."

"I told you I enjoy working with my hands," Benjamin said.

"You find yourself any oil?

Benjamin stopped to stare, and that pitted face hardened like asphalt setting. He crushed the empty Vienna can and strode away without answering.

They again worked late. When Chip left, he remembered he'd forgotten his thermos. He'd started bringing his own water. He left the pickup's engine running, and as he walked back toward the house, he glimpsed Benjamin out in the briar-tangled field beyond the old kitchen.

Benjamin leaned his weight on the galvanized pipe, his head bowed as if praying out there in the dusk. He must've sensed Chip 'cause he turned and stood straight. Chip got the thermos and drove off.

He told his mother about Benjamin being out in the

field. She'd kept dinner for Chip. She was tired from operating a stitching machine at the shoe factory but sat with him. She set her elbows on the table and cupped her chin in her palms.

"I been thinking about it," she said. "He got to have some connection with the Gatlin Place."

"Benjamin's a Jew name and no Jew ever lived out there," Chip's daddy said. He'd come from picking roasting ears in the backyard garden. Barefooted, he wore beltless Levi's and an undershirt. Corn pollen stuck to sweat along his arms.

"It's a Biblical name," the mother said. "Lots of them took or was given names from the Bible."

"Maybe so," Chip's daddy said, washing his hands at the sink. "They had got to get names somewheres."

"What happened to them?" Chip asked.

"Who?" his daddy asked and turned from the sink where he shucked ears of Silver Queen. The clean white kernels glistened.

"Those that got names," Chip said. "Must've been a bunch way back when to work all that tobacco."

"Many surely lived and died out there," his mama said, nodding.

"Hell, who knows or cares now?" his daddy said.

By late August they'd torn the house down, all of it, and filled the basement with what they'd pitched in. Benjamin hired Watkins Hendrick to bring his dozer to raze, flatten, and cover what was left with soil. When Watkins leveled off the house plot, Benjamin limed, fertilized, and seeded the area with Kentucky 31 fescue.

"You want me back for anything?" Chip asked. He'd been paid his exact wages as always with new bills.

"Keep the grass cut and your time," Benjamin said. "I'll send a monthly check. Bring a mower. I'll add a dollar fifty cents an hour for its use."

That's the last Chip saw of Mr. A. I. Benjamin. For a while after he left, there was bad talk around about his doings at the Gatlin place. Crazy, some said, hateful others. The sheriff should've stopped it. Except for Julius Temple Gatlin's courthouse portrait, no trace remained of what the family had meant to Howell County.

Chip lifted the Sears mower down from the pickup's tailgate and found Benjamin had demolished the old kitchen and all other outbuildings too. He next discovered what he first believed to be a gravestone planted at the center of the grassed-over plot. Bury a house?

If a grave marker, it had no writing or inscription. He thought maybe there could be a single letter and ran a finger into the grainy dip. Nope, it was just a flat upright brown fieldstone, lopsided, speckled with mica.

For three years he cut grass and received checks from a New York bank. By that time he'd gotten himself hired as an apprentice linesman for Virginia Power. The third autumn checks stopped coming, and a Lynchburg agent pounded a For Sale sign in the ground near the head of the cedar lane.

Chip still hunted the fields, the dogs not his daddy's but his own now he was married to Alice Anne and worked steady. Wind had long since blown loose posted signs along the fence, and strands of barb wire drooped and had gaps.

Buck and Snap stood a covey among the starved box bushes of the old formal garden. Honeysuckle, creeper, and cat brier dragged at them and were claiming everything back. Because of wildly flourishing weeds Chip could just make out the tilted markers and the rusted vine-tangled pickets of the Gatlin cemetery.

Crossing behind the house past where the well pump had been, he kicked up the dipper he'd never drunk from. Its handle was bent, the dented cup partly smashed. He tossed it to the ground and glanced once more at snaking tangles of thick wisteria vines hanging from the scaly, limb-heavy white oaks spaced around the overgrown house plot.

He called to the dogs but kept looking back till slash pines growing in a field where once broad-leaf tobacco gave itself up to the sun blocked his view. He felt an urge to retrieve something, a keepsake, maybe the dipper, carry it home. What the hell for? Might hold a story but no cooling water to quench any man's thirst.

He hitched up his britches and tightened his belt. He meant to find another covey before cold and darkness fully gathered to end the day.

BLOOD

Even sitting alone and not lifting a hand, Les sensed eyes. Or lying nights in the third-story bedroom of what Tobaccoton people referred to as a mansion, he imagined peering shapes drifting up from the orchard to his gabled window. He pulled covers over his face.

A sun-blasted Virginia Fourth of July, and Hector, the aged black owner of the grocery shanty beside the Norfolk Southern tracks, sold fireworks drawn illegally from beneath a wooden counter grooved a sandy tinge by the drag of countless fingers. The cherry-bomb special: twenty-five cents.

Les's plan was to bury the bomb under a battalion of blue regimented lead soldiers in the vegetable garden located between the house and the stable that had been converted to a garage. Eugene would plow the plot soon anyway for his fall seeding of turnip salad, collards, and mustards.

Les meant to holler and alert his mother, grandmother, and Aunt Clara to stand and watch from the latticed veranda. He'd wave the paper Stars and Bars bought at the Howell County Fair, give a rebel yell, and fire the cherry bomb.

The women had carried fried chicken, cole slaw, and potato salad to the Mount Olivet Presbyterian Church picnic. He stuffed himself before hurrying home and pinching up the quarter from the top drawer of his mother's chiffonier.

She saved her change in a porcelain saucer that had three white lilies painted at the bottom. He'd kept his plan secret and intended to pay back the money from an allowance earned weekly for mowing grass and trimming edges of the turtleback front walk.

He changed clothes and hurried to the battlefield. As he redeployed soldiers behind wind-downed oak branches split and zigzagged to look like rail fences, the women returned, and his mother called from a window of her white bedroom.

They waited for him. The top chiffonier drawer had been pulled out, and his mother held the porcelain saucer in her palms.

"Leslie, anything you wish to tell us?" she asked, a tall woman, erect, her dark hair graying, her eyes large and pale lavender. She rarely blinked, and when she did, it seemed an utterance.

"For god's sake it's only—" Aunt Clara said, younger than his mother, her sister. Aunt Clara had what his grandmother termed a weak chin, in fact hardly any chin at all. She often cupped a hand over it. Never married, she worked in the Commissioner's Office at the courthouse and smoked Lucky Strikes right down to her nicotined knuckles.

"Let him speak," Les's mother said, raising the saucer. She had on no jewelry, not a single ring. She did wear a small gold watch on a black silk cord looped around her neck. The watch once belonged to her maternal grandmother, whose husband had been a circuit court judge. Portraits hung in the parlor.

"Nobody home and I—" Les said.

"—took the money," his grandmother said. Age had shortened her, but she still held her back straight. As a child she'd worn a brace passed down to women of the family to insure good posture. She had white hair pulled into a bun, and her grape-blue eyes were recessed under thick brows. She sat in the window seat, her black shoes drawn tightly together.

"I got a show ready for you in the garden," Les said.

"You came into my room, opened my drawer, and took my money," his mother said.

"—a quarter," Aunt Clara said, lighting another unfiltered Lucky. She drew on cigarettes like a man, inhaling deep and shooting smoke through her nose. The grandmother couldn't object to tobacco odor in the house because the family's wealth had been made on the planting and sale of the dark-fired leaf to the Scandinavians.

Les's Great Uncle Benjamin had operated the brick warehouse at the south end of River Street where parallel rows of baskets got auctioned off in the midst of tawny, aroused dust. These days most local farmers carried their crop to Blackstone, and Uncle Benjamin's warehouse had been sold out of the family.

"Stealing's not quantity," Les's mother said. "It's an act of character."

"But I honest meant to pay it—" Les said.

"You must never, never do such a thing again," his mother said. She still held the saucer in her palms—like an offering before the altar at Mount Olivet.

He left the room feeling hot-faced and the eyes crawly on his back. He walked to the garden, dug up the cherry bomb, and carried it and the soldiers to the Hidden River.

He threw them into the brown, sluggish flow. The soldiers sank, and the cherry bomb floated away unlit. He furled the flag and left it in the basement that smelled of apples in the wooden bin.

Each fall he walked the lane at the front of the house to school. Burgundy leaves of overarching boughs dropped shade thick enough to be fingered. They were called the Victoria oaks because planted in 1837, the first year of that queen's reign. From a limb his father had hung a swing made by tying a length of raw hemp rope to a bald Goodrich tire. Eugene, his grandmother's yardman, had been ordered to cut it down.

When left alone at the house, Les searched. There were seven bedrooms and many more closets, most unused, yet still containing musty silk dresses, hats, and shoes the leather of which had dried and cracked. He wondered what'd happened to the brace.

He discovered three ivory-handled straight razors, spurs, a cane that had a bone handle carved like a fox head, a rusted .32-caliber Iver Johnson revolver, the cylinder empty of bullets, and a heavy calvary sword, its hilt battered, the blade deeply nicked.

No vestige of his father, not a snapshot, tie, or hairbrush. Disjointed impressions recurred—the tire swing and on the second-story veranda a hairy, muscular man laughing and naked to the waist, his arms raised to hold Les up to sunlight piercing thick foliage of the white oaks.

"He left," was the explanation, the words pronounced emphatically, Les's mother's face rigid in the pained, stricken manner assumed while she sat in the music room. She no longer played the Chickering, the lid of which she kept

closed so the western sun would not further yellow the
keys. A dried-up peacock's fan covered the fireplace, and
Ramona often failed to wind the Seth Thomas clock on the
marble mantel.

His tight-lipped grandmother told Les, "He squandered
her money." Nothing more.

Les questioned Ramona, the black maid young and full
bodied when she'd first arrived to work at the house. He'd
watched her raise her arms to hang clothes on the line, an
act that hoisted breasts that shifted mysteriously and appeared to have their own life. He felt guilt, but the stirring
did not quiet.

Now Ramona had mothered babies and become heavy
in hips and thighs, no longer walking lightly. He sat at the
kitchen table while she rolled out pie dough on the floured
counter. Eugene, bent and aching, had managed to pick a
quart of blood-red cherries in the orchard before crows and
grackles raided the tree.

"Don't ask me nothing," Ramona lowered her voice to
say and glanced toward the front of the house where Les's
grandmother talked with Mr. Hampton Waters from the
Planter's Bank. Grandfather Clifford had been a founder,
and Mr. Waters, now president, personally brought the
monthly check. The grandmother served him tea in her
second-best china.

"But you seen," Les whispered to Ramona, who kept her
back to him. She wore a green uniform that had a white
V collar.

"I seen and that's all. Your mamma kill me if she knew I
talking. Be smoke and blood all over this place. How I remember? He just another man gone."

A blazing, June afternoon, school let out for the summer

and a day sweet with freedom. While Les and Skeeter Tuck fished for crappie, Buck Mosley, who worked at the Brookneal chenille plant, stopped his yolk-yellow Cougar above the riverbank. The Cougar sported mag rims, dual carburetors, and a pounding tape deck. He kept that mean machine shiny as a licked lemon sucker.

Lou Brightwell stepped out to stand beside him. She wore tight red shorts and a yellow tank top. Les and Skeeter were obliged to accept an offered Bud from the iced six-pack or have their manhood shamed in front of bold, red-headed Lou. Many nights Les had pictured her high-stepping it in gold boots and flashing the white insides of her thighs. Half the boys in Tobaccoton lusted after Lou, whose father and mother had jobs at the shoe factory.

Carl Whitlock, a county deputy, happened to be driving over the one-lane plank bridge and saw the glints off the beer cans. He parked among sycamores to sneak to the riverbank. Carl, a Baptist, asked Les and Skeeter their ages. Skeeter had turned eighteen and was legally cleared. Les fell a year short.

"Could write you a ticket but I'll just let your folks know what you up to," Carl said.

Eyes again, this time in the dusky front parlor with its heavy damask curtains and murky portraits. His mother and grandmother sat him before them on a pink velvet chair that had polished brass knobs for feet.

"I hardly swallowed," Les said. "I just held the can."

"And the girl, Lou Brightwell, you know her reputation in this town," his mother said.

"They drove up after Skeeter and me were fishing," Les said. "She's Buck's girl."

"What we hear she's everybody's," his grandmother said,

she seated in a winged leather chair set under the portrait of Great-Grandfather Boyd dressed in black judicial robes.

"I hated the taste," Les said. "I spit it out."

"*Spat*," his mother said and clasped her hands. "Go to your room."

His punishment was Moultrie Military Academy down in Georgia. Exile denied him his junior and senior years at John Randolph High School. He didn't mind the rigid life and hazing much as he was used to obeying rules. His flesh quickly absorbed bruises from cadet officers' ratting blows and the saber canings laid on with the flat of the blades.

Lots of city boys from the North, more worldly and streetwise, a few scary bad, like a leering weasel from East Orange, New Jersey, who poured gasoline on a cat and set it afire. The big things Les learned had nothing to do with textbooks and discipline.

Vacations he wore his uniform home and found himself invited to parties. After the Toetappers Cotillion it was he caught Aunt Clara. He'd been allowed to drive his mother's Chrysler to carry Betsy Anne Bowser to the dance. Got not even a belly rub from yakking, giggly Betsy and only a single tight-mouth goodnight kiss at her lighted doorway.

Instead of heading straight home, Les wound back through the still, silent town where electric Christmas candles burned in windows and a spotlight struck through darkness to illuminate the eerie crèche before the spired, ghostly Mount Olivet Church.

He cruised along what locals called the Hanging Tree Road. He realized he'd better not have an accident or he'd need to explain what he was doing out in the sticks instead of coming straight home. What he was doing was thinking of Lou Brightwell and feeling himself up.

He pulled into a fire trail dividing a two-hundred-acre stand of loblollies belonging to the Georgia Pacific Company, and the sweeping headlights uncovered Aunt Clara and Mr. Douglas Gaffney. Mr. Gaffney, the county commissioner, hopped around jerking at his trousers as Aunt Clara slid from the Chevette's hood to shove down her skirt. Their faces gleamed white as cemetery gravestones.

Les drove home where he lay in bed and heard Aunt Clara's car roll in slow and soft along the lane. He figured they'd used the hood because the interior of her Chevette was too cramped for maneuvering. Mr. Douglas Gaffney's wife Bernice sang in the Mount Olivet choir and had born him three daughters.

Aunt Clara slipped through the side entrance and up the back stairs. Les cracked his bedroom door and leaned out to listen to her fading, swishing footsteps on the hall carpet. The house still smelled of cedar from the decorated tree Eugene had taken down and hauled out to burn.

Saturday morning Aunt Clara ate no breakfast, and he didn't see her again till that night when she sat across from him at the oak table that'd belonged to Great-Grandfather Paulson. With all its leaves in place the table seated twelve people and still allowed room for elbow flapping. Aunt Clara knew he sneaked looks at her as she spooned her rice soup. She reddened but never glanced at Les.

He knocked on her door later. She rarely joined his mother and grandmother in the upstairs den. Her bedroom, like his, was in the rear, though on the second floor and perfumed. She'd propped herself among pillows on her blue chaise to read *Mademoiselle*.

Her table radio played country rock from a Blackstone station. Les caught the quick dip of her hand to the far side of the chaise. He'd discovered she kept a washed highball glass in her room and hid her vodka on the bookshelf behind a copy of *Miss Manners' Guide to Excruciatingly Correct Behavior.* Her hand cupped her chin, and again she blushed.

"You ratting on me?" she asked, smoke coiling around her words. She reached to switch off the radio.

"Trade you," he said. She'd arranged her antique doll collection on the window seat that covered an iron radiator. All the prettily dressed dolls sat sweet and smiling beneath panes blackened by night and rattled by wind.

"Trade me what?" she asked. Despite her lack of chin, she had lustrous short brown hair and kindly brown eyes. She looked real nice when she took time to primp. She must've gussied up to attract Mr. Douglas Gaffney, who wouldn't've needed to think about her chin out there under the loblollies.

"Don't just tell me my father left," Les said.

She closed her magazine, swung her feet to the floor, and snubbed out her Lucky in a seashell. Though her fingernails had no polish, she'd painted her toenails red. She pushed at her hair and ran fingers down her throat before flipping her pearl-colored negligee over plump knees. She shook her head.

"What'd he do so bad I can't get answers?" Les asked.

She looked up at him from the tops of her eye sockets.

"Some things are better not found out," she said.

"Guess you'd know about that."

"All right, damn you for being a sneak, he walked out on a Boyd. Nobody in the entire history of this illustrious family had ever before done such an unheard of, despicable thing."

"Why'd he do the walking?"

"Wasn't born in Tobaccoton or even Virginia. Rolled down here from the West Virginia mountains, used the wrong fork, and you know how an act of such world-shaking importance is received around this place. Your father stole your mother, swept her off her feet at the Tobacco Festival. He was passing through on his way to a construction job in Tennessee and attracted by the lanterns and street-dancing music."

Aunt Clara stood and crossed to her dresser mirror. She edged her face sideways to inspect herself but still kept the chin covered.

"Your mother suffered a moment of weakness," she said. "He was terrible handsome in a rawboned fashion. Black hair, big shoulders, slab-faced. They didn't get married in church but a roadside chapel by a quickie preacher up in Maryland. Drove her car and used her money to pay that preacher. Good thing Daddy lay in the grave. He'd have shot Morgan. Mamma like to died."

Morgan, his father's given name not spoken in the house.

"Got to be more," Les said.

"Your daddy was about as popular around here as a coon in the corn crib," she said and returned to the chaise where she sat and stared at her feet. "Didn't set any records for working hard at Uncle Benjamin's warehouse. Liked a drink or two. I'll say this—he brought the house alive."

"Keep going."

"You sure you want to hear everything?"

"I am."

She lit a Lucky, took a drag deep enough to reach her red toenails, and snorted smoke. A corner of her mouth twisted up.

"You were already on the way," she said. "Before the trip to Maryland."

Les had to think a second before he understood. Then shame pumped hot as he remembered his mother's words *act of character.* Was that the reason they'd been watching him over the years, to see his father in him, fearing or expecting conduct exposing a taint of genes?

"They ran him off?" Les asked.

"More like Morgan was a leper. People in the house and around town looking down on him. He got to drinking heavy and became sick."

"Sick how?" Les asked, hope rising because there'd been much sickness in the family and that was acceptable and required no guilt or repentance.

Aunt Clara hesitated. She drew on the Lucky, sighed, shook her head.

"Tell it," Les said.

"Kind men catch from women they shouldn't be out with."

She closed her eyes, and he pictured colored illustrations bright as intestines from a cut hog on pages of the hygiene chapter in the ROTC Manual at Moultrie Military. He recalled dirty, snickering remarks made by fellow cadets.

"I didn't want to tell you," Aunt Clara said.

"Where'd he go?" Les asked.

"Back to the mountains. A little coal town. Bear Paw as I remember." She dropped the hand from her chin. "Oh, Leslie, unwanted, lonely people do odd and hurting things. Try to understand and forgive."

During Christmas break his second year at Moultrie Military, Les's grandmother gave him a new fifty-dollar bill in a Planter's Bank envelope decorated with red-berried holly leaves. He also saved a cut of his weekly allowance doled out by Colonel Evers. By April Les had eighty-seven dollars held back.

His mother expected him home for Easter. He chanced she wouldn't know exactly when his vacation started. He lopped off the first two of ten days and wrote to tell her he'd be coming on Monday, April 17.

Instead of taking Amtrack from Atlanta to Richmond and the bus to Tobaccoton, he carried his bag to the Greyhound depot in Moultrie, rode it first to Charlotte, then Roanoke, and finally through the night to Bear Paw in southern West Virginia.

Day dawned as the Greyhound stopped before a peeling white clapboard store that had two self-service gasoline pumps in front and an overhang porch with a bench three old men sat on. The driver handed Les his bag and pulled away fast, leaving oily, stringy dark diesel fumes strung along the shadowed valley.

Snow patched wooded slopes, which rose on each side of Bear Paw. Roads branching off the one paved street were cindered. A stream ran through town, sluicing full from melting snow. A coal drag banged, rattled, and clanged past, the hopper cars empty. Dogs barked. On the mountainside a small narrow church had suffered wind damage, its steeple tilted.

Toting his bag, Les climbed the porch steps. The store also served as the post office, and a flag hung over the entrance. On one side of the screened double door an Honest Snuff sign had been tacked to siding. At the other a tin Orange Crush bottle displayed a thermometer embedded at the center. It read sixty-seven degrees.

Legs crossed, the three men on the bench stopped chewing to watch him from flinty probing eyes. Two mossbacks were bearded, and all wore high-top shoes, leather jackets, checkered wool shirts buttoned to the collar, and billed caps.

"Morning," Les said. They continued to gaze as if they hadn't heard. Maybe it was his uniform. He sidled into the store.

Open wooden shelves stretched back into dimness where a single light bulb burned. Salt-cured hams dangled from rafters, their scent sharp. Mounted deer looked down, dusty eyes shocked and sad. A set of antlers cradled a lever-action rifle, the dangling price tag attached to the trigger guard. A thin, white-haired man wearing an apron and black leather bow tie stood behind a crank type cash register.

"Looking for somebody who might live 'round here," Les said.

"Might covers lots of territory," the man said. He was toothless, gums anemic, his accent different from Virginia or Georgia, higher in the nose, the words bitten off.

"Name of Sharp. Hoping you know of him."

"Hope don't cost a dime," the man answered. He reset his glasses. The three who'd been sitting on the porch bench filed in. They'd come to watch and listen. "They's always Sharps."

"Morgan Sharp," Les said. "From Bear Paw."

"Chances if he be from, he was and gone," the storekeeper said. "And gone means ain't."

"Maybe you heard of him."

"Maybes cover lots of territory too," the storekeeper said and spit—spat—aside into a five-gallon lard can partly filled with black soil.

"Any you gentlemen able to help?" Les asked, turning to the men at the door.

"Son, this is a dying town," the storekeeper said, tearing open a carton of Brown's Mule to arrange plugs in a glass-front case that needed wiping. "Most coal's mined out, and most people is too. Just a few left up-holler. Soon won't be nothing left but crows and cockroaches."

Les still held his bag. He stood uncertain what to do next. He hadn't eaten breakfast and looked at the candy bars in the display case. He bought a Hershey almond. Possibly somebody in the town remembered. As he passed the three men and opened the door, one spoke:

"Sheila Ackers," he said. "She knew Morgan."

"Who she didn't?" a second man said.

"How do I find Miss Ackers?" Les asked.

"Miss, huh?" the first said.

"Up the street," the second man said.

"The old bank," the third said. "Steps at the side."

Les thanked them and changing hands on his bag left the store. The wan sunlight shone through haze. Weeds flourished from cracks in the broken concrete sidewalk.

Buildings had been boarded up, a furniture outlet offered a mattress sale, and a sign soaped across the window of a grocery store advertised pork ribs. A man wearing rubber boots hosed off used cars in a lot strung with motionless red-white-and-blue whirligigs. Everywhere the alien, lingering scent of coal.

Les ate his Hershey as he walked. A skinny tow-headed young boy bumped his bicycle across railroad tracks. Two men wearing miners' helmets passed in a grimy Ford pickup, their faces blackened except for masklike whiteness around the eyes.

The keystone of the brick two-story bank had a date on it—1928. Cinder block had been used to mortar up windows. The steps at the side were a rusted iron fire escape.

Les climbed to a studded metal door that had a dried Christmas wreath hanging from a knocker shaped like a miner's pick. The knocker was hinged at the handle end. He heard music. His stomach pressed up a vomity almond taste.

When he raised and let the knocker fall, the wreath dropped to bars of the deck. As he lifted the wreath, the door opened and he faced a hefty woman dressed in a flowered housecoat and carpet slippers. She had frizzy yellow hair. She held a blue-eyed Siamese cat and saucer of cream. The cat struggled to reach the saucer.

"You not Buster," she said and set the cat and saucer inside on the floor. The cat lapped milk but watched Les.

"No'm," he said and rehung her shedding wreath. "My name's Leslie Sharp, and I rode the bus to Bear Paw to find my father Morgan of the same name."

Her eyes were pale green, the lids faintly tinted. On her fingers she wore rings, many with stones, others ordinary, one made from a bent horseshoe nail. She settled a spread hand on a poked-out hip and looked him up and down. Her body gave off a whiff of perfume.

"Well don't it beat all?" she said. "You sure God got to be the calling card he left."

"The men at the store told me you knew him."

"They done did, did they? Well they right for once. Come on in, boy. Coffee on the stove."

Despite the building's sooty, forsaken exterior, the room he entered was clean, bright, and warm—a peach-colored sofa with a patch quilt draped over the back, a La-Z-Boy chair, a color TV, phantom figures dancing around on the screen.

Her rear window looked out to the mountainside and a blackened tipple. Snapshots had been tacked to walls. A large painting on black satin of Willie Nelson holding a banjo, his face giving off sunbeams and favoring Jesus hung above an oil heater piped into a bricked-up fireplace.

Les set down his bag. Beyond a multicolored beaded curtain a kitchen held a modern GE stove and refrigerator. Coffee boiled in a pot that had no lid.

"Hobo style," she said, taking from the shelf a heavy white mug, the kind he'd drunk from in the Mess Hall at Moultrie Military. "Way real men like it."

"I'm hoping you can tell me where to find him," Les said. The cat continued to lap and watch.

"You asking the wrong person about that," she said, poured the coffee, and handed him the mug. She turned down the TV before she sat on the sofa by releasing her heavy body the last few inches. She toppled backwards, and her slippered feet raised an instant before she balanced herself and set them back on a floor partly covered by a circular rag rug. "Morgan ain't been 'round here since I wore a miniskirt. But sit yourself."

Les did, on a cane rocking chair that squeaked and crackled under and behind him. The mug's hotness burned his palms.

"My you nice looking in that uniform," she said. "Morgan wore a uniform too and was handsome as any soldier who ever paraded the colors. Had all the gals in heat, including me. War ruined him. Made him such a hell-raiser. Couldn't hold a job. Couldn't hold nothing much but a bottle and, well, a couple of other things."

"Appreciate it if you'd tell me more about him," Les said. The building trembled as another empty coal drag passed on rails behind the building.

"I can tell you I was likely his last friend 'round here," she said. "After the fight that knocked out a side at the Red Dog Tavern, he had to make tracks. Left so fast his wind pulled trees after him. Went west somewhere. Got a card from Colorado a long time ago. Picture of cliffs where cave dwellers once lived."

"He ever talk about me?" Les asked and despite the mug's heat gripped it hard.

"Sure did. Wanted to go back and see you, but the law and lawyers was after him. Tried to call you on the phone. Nobody at the house would let you talk. They used him bad down in old Virginia."

"You think he's alive?"

"Might could be out 'er," she said. The cat finished its milk and jumped to her lap. She stroked it. "Had lots of life in him. Then again it's been a spell and him living ninety miles an hour. Just don't know."

Les drank, stood, and set the cup on an end table that held fanned *TV Guides*. He thanked her. She heaved up off the sofa, the cat limp over an arm. He looked at snapshots along the wall.

"None of your daddy," she said. "But like to see how pretty I was a hundred years ago?"

She pointed a scarlet fingernail at the picture of a young woman wearing a pink bathing suit and standing by an ivy-covered sundial in a garden of blooming roses. She was stout even then, but pretty, smiling, a hand lifted, a knee bent in the way women will.

"One thing I might still got," she said. She waddled into

a windowless room where she switched on a ceiling light and rooted around in dresser drawers. The double bed's purple comforter gave off a sheen.

"Ah yeah," she said and crossed out to him. Les recognized the combat infantryman's badge. The drill instructor at Moultrie Military wore his pinned to his uniform. This one Miss Ackers held had been fused to a narrow, curved rectangular strip of steel and linked by a catch and wrist chain to make a bracelet. "Morgan pounded, drilled, and welded it himself."

She laid it on Les's palm. The metal felt cool and substantial. All but a speck of bluish paint around the tarnished emblematic musket had worn or flaked away.

"Went kind of crazy when he came back but was a brave man," she said. "Had his name in the Beckley paper. Before he met your mamma. You keep it. Don't mean nothing to me now, and my wrist's too thick. But, listen, I always liked your daddy. Even after he turned wild, I knew he had good in him."

Les stood holding the bracelet and thanked her. She leaned to and kissed his cheek before opening the door. She called to him he'd forgotten his bag.

"You locate him, you tell him Sheila said hello."

Nodding, lightheaded, he walked down the chiming steps and back along the street empty of people to the store where the three old men again sat on the bench.

"Find anything?" one asked.

"Something," Les said and lowered himself to an up-ended Nehi crate at the other end of the porch. He relaxed his fingers to view the bracelet. He wiped it on his pants. Maybe brass button polish would shine it up.

He rode the bus to Roanoke, Lynchburg, and Tobaccoton. It was past midnight when he lugged his bag up the lane under the overhanging great oaks, whose shapes loomed as darkness within darkness. Windows were lighted, and in the parlor waited his mother, grandmother, Aunt Clara, the sheriff, the preacher, and Colonel Evers, commandant from Moultrie Military.

Les leveled his eyes at them. He didn't touch but sensed the heft of the bracelet carried in the left-hand breast pocket of his uniform jacket.

Somewhere in the west . . .

LANDINGS

William was a sorry thing for a man—scrawny, fish-belly white, head jerking around on a skinny neck like he believed somebody was about to jump him. During late April while the Chesapeake's waters still held March's cold, he rented a ramshackle summer cottage set on bowed piling at Winter Harbor.

I eyed him from my skiff as I ran crab pots. He sat in a canvas beach chair on the cottage's deck. I waved, but he didn't lift a hand to answer.

He bought groceries at the Little Sue store in Port Haven, mostly canned goods when strawberries and cresses were in season and snaps, peaches, tomatoes, and sweet corn coming on. He was a heater, not a cooker, and it's no wonder he looked sickly.

He wore khakis and didn't roll up his shirt sleeves even on days when the blistering sun turned the air so wavy you believed your brain had boiled. He spoke as if each word cost him big money.

"Look," I told him in the Little Sue parking lot as he ducked into a rusting black Beetle that had no bumpers and a fender bashed off, "there's fresh vegetables all around and a world of food right out there for free in the bay. You catch a flounder, eat the meat, put the shuckings in a pot, haul in crabs, feed on the lump and backfin, bait a minnow trap with what's left, use the shiners to hook more fish, and you got yourself a perpetual motion feeding machine."

"Wonderful," he said. That's all. He didn't hardly look at me. He was younger than he carried himself, mid-twenties at most, his sandy hair needing scissors. Being short, pug-nosed, and freckled like all the women in Mama's family, I had no claim to beauty, but I had naturally curly red hair, blue eyes, and never a pimple in my entire life.

William wore sunglasses that had black lenses. I thought he might be reading on his deck, but when I looked through my nocs across the harbor, he never held a book or magazine.

Monday evening making a run in from setting a gill net in the bay, I cut my engine and coasted toward reeds bordering his property.

"Hey, come on, I'll take you for a ride," I called. I'd asked his name at the post office. It was William J. Cabell.

He sat without moving.

"Won't cost you a dime," I hollered.

He stood, walked down the steps from his deck, and slouched among tangled, knee-high saw grass to the water's edge. He was so skinny half a gale'd carry him off.

"I'll teach you the harbor," I said. "Keep you from going aground on the mudflats."

"I don't intend ever to be on the harbor or mudflats either," he said and turned back toward the cottage.

"You could thank me for the offer," I called after him, jerked the starter rope on my twenty-five-horsepower Evinrude, and throttled her full. I left him the wash of my wake.

I never again meant to have anything to do with him. Let him sit and waste away till kingdom come. For a couple of days I didn't look in his direction when I made my runs. Saturday I just happened to slide my eyes toward his cottage. He wasn't sitting in the chair but sprawled face down on the deck. Well, I thought, he's either sunning himself or rusted out.

I ran my skiff ashore, set the anchor, and brushed through swamp elder to the cottage. Paint had weathered off and roof shingles blowed away by nor'easters. Torn screens made him skeeter bait.

He lay with a cheek against the deck, his mouth hanging open. I knelt and found him still breathing. I couldn't call the Rescue Squad 'cause William had no phone. As I towed him by his arms into shade, I uncovered the bottle of Aristocrat vodka.

Disgusted, I let him drop, and he thumped back to the deck. Wasting my time on a drunk. His shirttail had pulled out, and under it I first thought he wore ladylike underwear.

I lifted the shirt. Not underwear. A scar like pink silk covered his back. He'd been burned, and the scar's sleekness ran from the top of his shoulders to down below his belt.

Gently as I could I drew him inside. He'd been using a cot with a thin mattress, and the sheets needed changing. I smoothed the bottom one before settling him on it.

The cot, a card table with spindly legs, and the beach chair was all the furniture he owned. He'd dropped clothes on the floor and let them lie. Ants trooped across the iron-stained sink where bean and sardine cans had been tossed. Dirty paper plates spilled from a plastic garbage bag. Flies spiraled around it and me.

I couldn't just leave him there for the skeeters to feed on.

He wouldn't have no blood left. I found a can of OFF in a cabinet over the cruddy stove and sprayed him down good before draping the top sheet over him.

I figured while I was there I might as well clean up the kitchen and smelly bathroom. He did have Comet and steel wool, which I used on the stove and sinks. From a ceiling light fixture I knocked down a dirt-dauber nest and swept the broken pieces out the back door.

As I was fixing to leave, he licked his lips, groaned, and set a hand over his eyes.

"Jesus, what a stink," he said.

"It's your own living like a pig," I said.

He reared slowly to an elbow. He had nice eyes, honey brown, but buried in them a terrible fear. I'd seen the same expression in the dying look from a buck I shot in the marsh. William worked his bare feet to the floor.

"Who asked you?" he said and pushed at his ratty hair.

"I don't need to be asked. I'd help a run-over dog on the highway."

"This not a highway."

"But you a dog," I said and left him sitting on the edge of the cot looking gaunt and wasted.

My given name was Jennette, though around the harbor people called me Punch because of a fight I had in the tenth grade at Bayside High. A boy named Scrooch was beating up on another student named Dork who weighed about half as much, and when I yanked Scrooch off by the ear and told him to quit, he laughed and pinched my nose. I socked him dead square on his chin. He stumbled back, fell, and his legs shot up. Dusting hisself, he stood, saying, "I ain't fighting no girl."

I didn't mind the name so much back then, was even proud of it for I was still mostly tomboy, but my senior year at parties and dances, I wanted to be called Jennette. Because of my stubby figure and the fact I liked working on the water, the boys considered me rough and rugged. I didn't get to do much dancing.

Truth is I had a load of softness in me. It was more than Jesus and membership in the Ebenezer Baptist Church. When I was a little girl, I watched a young osprey hook his claws into a chopper. He got dragged down under the water and drownded. I buried that bird in a sand dune and mourned his beauty gone to a clot of matted feathers. I cried lots inside where people couldn't see.

I thought of William Cabell living by himself, all scarred, drinking liquor, eating out of cans, lonely, afraid. On July 4 my Christian duty prompted me to bake a fresh loaf of Sally Lunn and a crab casserole, boil up a mess of greens, and brew a gallon jar of iced tea to carry over to him in my cooler.

When I knocked on his screen door, he didn't answer it. I walked around front to the deck, and he sat wearing the sunglasses, though it was a gray day, the nimbus clouds hanging low and fat.

"Brought you a decent meal," I said.

"I've eaten," he said.

"I know how you eat."

I lowered the food to the deck, walked inside, and lifted out the card table. After wiping it with a paper towel, I placed it over his legs. When I set the meal before him, he pushed away from it.

"Try some of my famous crab casserole," I said.

"Don't like crustaceans of any sort."

"You'll love this dish," I said and unwrapped the fork, knife, and spoon I'd brought. I peeled the aluminum foil from the casserole, dipped out a bite, and held it in front of his mouth. He took it in and spit it out, splattering my new white blouse. I smacked him so hard his sunglasses fell off.

He sat jarred, his arms hanging over the sides of the chair. I fed him another spoonful of casserole. He mouthed it and watched me, his face shrunk back. Oh God, his honey eyes were so hurt and frightened. It was more terrible than the ugly scar on his body. He had to be all pain inside.

"We gonna put meat on you," I said and wiped his mouth with the napkin I'd brought, cloth not paper. He kept drawing away in the chair each time I reached the spoon to him.

"How'd I get myself into this fuckup?" he asked.

"You want another whacking, keep talking dirty," I said and set the sunglasses over his eyes.

"Yes, Boss," he said. "Just don't whip up on me again."

I didn't carry William food every day, only once or twice a week. I'd sit on his deck steps and talk to him whether he answered or not.

"Crabs running good," I said. "Course that drags the price down. Jimmys selling for about forty-five dollars a bushel now. Close to sixty early in the season."

"Jimmys?" he asked. His first word to me that still hot evening. Rails cackled in the marsh, and hulls of work boats squeaked against piling along the public dock.

"Male crabs. The ladies are sooks. Not as much meat, maybe a third less. Bring a lower price and that's by the barrel, not the bushel. Two and a half bushels to a barrel.

Some are cushions, or spongers, laying their eggs. Feel sorry for them. After they release the eggs, they go off and die. Like they willingly give up the ghost."

"Crabs don't have ghosts," he said.

"I believe everything has ghosts. Fish too, though not netting much right now. Used to haul tubs of white perch, but they gone. Taking a few trout, blues, croakers, and spot are beginning to run. Don't get much for choppers. Lucky to bring ten cent a pound. Cull a few peelers I sell to tourist hook-and-line fishermen."

"Fascinating," William said.

"You watch it," I said.

"You think ticks and spiders have ghosts? How about sharks and crocodiles?"

"There's good and bad ghosts."

"Thanks for straightening that out for me," he said.

Often he'd go to sleep while I was talking. I'd slip off to my skiff and cross the moon-striped harbor home.

"Notice you cooking up a storm these days," my daddy said. He was nearly as broad as tall, heavy boned, big hands. He drove to Newport News each morning to work at the shipyard. He'd been a waterman but gave up the life for regular pay and turned over his skiff to me, one he'd planked not ten feet from our dock. He still had biceps that'd lump up hard as Irish 'taters.

"You keeping score on what I do?" I asked. He was teasing but had to know my tender feelings on the subject of men.

"Need to sharpen my pencil for that," he said.

My face burned. I'd not had a real boyfriend in my whole life, and I wasn't thinking of William Cabell like that. I meant it about helping run-over dogs. William across the harbor was practically a neighbor, and neighbors had responsibilities to each other.

I again stopped by the Port Haven post office and talked to Lester Cragget, postmaster, who also worked the window.

"Anybody ever write William Cabell?" I asked.

"Can't reveal that information," Lester said—young, full of hisself at the got-it-made government job he'd been appointed to. Other candidates had been older and more deserving, but his uncle was brother-in-law to a congressman. "That's the man's private business."

"Private isn't everything," I said. "Might take you gunning come duck time."

"Never met a blackie or honker I didn't like," Lester said, glanced around, and lowered his voice as if a postal inspector might be listening. "Uncle Sam sends Mr. William J. Cabell a monthly pension check. He also gets longhand letters from Richmond. He comes for his checks. He chucks everything else in the trash can. Hasn't been here for almost three weeks."

"Let's see a letter," I said.

"Can't do that," he said, reaching to a pigeonhole and laying an envelope on the counter. "Against regulations. Course how'm I to stop you from looking if my back is turned, which it is right now."

I pulled the envelope to me. On it I read the sender's name, W. J. Cabell, II. A man's writing. I copied the return address on a vinyl siding advertisement I pulled from the trash. As I left the post office, up drove Lester's wife, Rita Doe. I admit she had a cute figure and might even be considered pretty with her dark hair frizzed up. She had on tight red shorts and a red halter that surely verged on being spilled over.

"Well, Punch, hear you finally hooked you some kind of a fish," she said and grinned.

She didn't mind showing her boobs or bitchiness. She drove all the way to Hampton to get her braces adjusted. I might never be cute as Rita Doe, but I kept myself clean and healthy. A lot to be said for that. And I'd never used eye shadow either or stuck a horse bit in my mouth to land a man.

"I don't expect anybody without brains to figure out how dumb they are," I answered her.

"Hope he likes *eau de* crab bait," she said and prissed on in the post office to see Lester and probably ask for money. I near ran after her to remind her how I got my nickname.

That night in my room I wrote to Mr. W. J. Cabell, II, at the Richmond address. I explained I didn't mean to be butting into his business, but I was a neighbor to William and he appeared troubled and I wondered could I do anything to help out. Careful of my penmanship, I also checked my spelling twice.

I mailed the letter Tuesday. Wednesday afternoon while I tarred crab pots, the dark green Caddy drove in behind our house, a white bungalow set on two acres of land lying along the harbor's south shore. Tourist, I thought. Maybe wanted peelers.

The man who stepped out was tall and thin, his hair silver gray. He wore a tan suit, white shirt, and pale blue tie. I wiped my hands with a rag dipped in gasoline and crossed the lawn to him. He had a narrow, kindly face.

"You the Miss Jennette who wrote the letter?" he asked and I knew this was William's father 'fore he spoke a word and that he'd turn out to be a cultured gentleman. They had the same long noses and outswept chins.

"Like a swallow of sweet tea?" I asked. Both my parents peeked out the kitchen window.

"That'd be nice," Mr. Cabell said.

We sat on the shaded bench Daddy had built by nailing 8" × 10' planks between two cedar trees. Blue jays fussed above us for disturbing their territory.

"It's kind of you to take an interest in my son," Mr. Cabell said, talking slow and soft. His hands were slim, and he wore a gold wedding band.

"He's not eating right and been drinking hard," I said.

"He's had trouble finding himself since his discharge from the hospital," Mr. Cabell said and told me his son got hurt not in Vietnam but while learning to be a Navy pilot and crashed the trainer on top a Florida high-voltage power line. Sparks'd ignited the fuel that burned him. He'd laid in the hospital eighteen months and received seven skin grafts.

"Afterwards he lived at home with us a time," Mr. Cabell said. "Refused to allow his friends to visit. He had a girl he wouldn't see. She's now engaged."

Mr. Cabell raised a veined hand to the side of his face and turned toward the harbor to try to keep me from seeing his teary eyes.

"He's bitter at the Navy, who ruled the crash pilot error, and also at his parents, whom he believes hadn't prepared him for what he calls 'the real world.' Our values seem false and hypocritical to him. When he moved out, we traced him through the Veterans Administration. The situation's causing my wife great distress."

"You going over to see him?"

"He'll not want to see me," Mr. Cabell said and ran a shaky palm over his finely combed hair. "If you'd be good enough to keep us informed. Call anytime, reverse the charges."

He gave me a card, William J. Cabell, II, Virginia Investor Associates, James River Plaza, Richmond. With his pen he wrote the home phone number on the back. I guessed William across the harbor was a III.

I walked him to his car and watched him drive away down our lane.

I'd considered entering nurse's training and thought about taking a secretarial course. Truth is I had outdoors in my blood. Six generations of my kin had lived beside the big water. Might as well hit me over the head with a sledge as stick me between walls under a roof.

I supported myself crabbing, gillnetting, and during winter tonging oysters, the few that were left. Being the only female waterman around the harbor caused talk. Men believed I'd never be able to stand up to gales' shrieking winds that'd rip hair off a cat.

I took lots of kidding around the docks, but they found I could ride wild water with the best of 'em. I made my way, bought my food, clothes, gear, and paid a weekly rent to my folks. I guess most men had forgot I was a woman.

I'd tried wearing a pair of high heels only once in my life and near broke an ankle. I tossed them into the Goodwill collection box. I still dabbed on a whiff of perfume evenings after striping down my boots, washing up, and drawing on clean Levi's, but the only wolf whistles I got were in fun.

Tuesday morning when I motored out to pull and rebait

my pots, William stood near the water's edge. Unusual to see him using his feet. He wore the sunglasses. I waved and drifted the boat into shore. Despite the raw sticky air, he still wore his khakis buttoned up.

"Come on," I said. "You afraid of getting wet?"

"What I'm afraid of is people who don't respect others' privacy."

"That's me. Better become used to it. Climb in and I'll give you the tour."

I didn't believe he would, but he stepped forward carefully through the reeds, climbed aboard, and sat athwart facing me. I shoved off and started the engine. I backed us out slow so the water pump wouldn't suck mud.

When I throttled forward, the rush of air felt cool and cleansing. My skiff lifted on plane. Scoggins strutted along the marsh's green edge. We rode from the harbor into the bay, which was slick calm, sunlight flickering and flashing off lazily rolling swells. Clam boats moved out, leaving behind expanding wakes. I waved to the cap'ns. Laughing gulls squawked over us, and terns dived and splashed.

Ospreys that'd nested on channel markers gave their sissylike cries, though no sissies themselves. The old birds acted like worried parents as their young left the nest and learned what wings were meant for.

"The kids fly pretty good right now, but they don't know how to land," I said.

"Yeah, always the landings," William said.

I realized I'd made a mistake and shut up. I had two lines of pots, forty in all, and I nosed in downwind, geared to neutral, and stood to gaff floats. I emptied the pots into the skiff and rebaited using frozen menhaden bought at Billup's Dock.

I separated sooks from jimmies, measuring and culling out illegals to toss over the side. William sat with his hands hanging between his knees and looked out toward the Eastern Shore, it distant and hazy. I guessed he was looking. You couldn't ever be sure because of the sunglasses.

A plane passed low, a military jet traveling to Oceana Air Base. Its wings gave off glints. William didn't raise his eyes and sat hunched as if being rained on.

I wore neoprene work gloves as much for stinging nettles as the crabs. Tentacles scummed pot lines. I did my best to keep my hands nice. Nights I rubbed them with Oil of Olay and for a time had painted my nails but they looked so out of place among the foul-talking rowdies at Billup's Dock I gave up doing that.

"You can help if you want," I said to William.

"Don't want."

"You ever have any visitors except me?" I asked, thinking I might get him to talk about his folks.

"Not when I'm lucky."

"What you got against people?"

"Being people," he said.

When I'd pulled my pots and was headed in, I accidentally knocked my coffee thermos over the side. It bobbed away. As I hove to on the guinea stick, William kicked off his unlaced tennis shoes, dived into the water, and disappeared. God, I believed he was committing suicide.

He splashed up right under the thermos, caught it, and stuffed it under his chin to swim back to the skiff—not dog-paddling but overhand, the strokes slow and graceful.

He grabbed the gunnel and lifted his chin over the side so I could take the thermos, then tried to haul himself aboard but sank back to the water. I reached to help him.

"Just wait a damn minute and I'll do it," he said. Again he didn't want me touching him.

"Where'd you learn to swim like that?" I asked. He still clung to the skiff, and I was glad he had his pants and shirt on so nettles couldn't much sting him.

"Never learned to swim like that," he said.

"What you mean? I just saw you."

"An illusion. Trick of the mind."

"That don't make sense," I said. "I mean doesn't."

"That's right, correct your grammar, and it'll carry you far in this life," he said as he struggled to climb over the gunnel. He got a leg raised, and when his pants pulled up, I saw more scar that looked like pink plastic. He worked the rest of his body across and tumbled to the deck. Bent and blowing, he pushed to his knees.

"I never learned to swim," I said, resisting the urge to steady him.

"You make your living on the water and never learned to swim?" he asked and looked at me like I was coot crazy.

"Not many watermen can. My parents can't."

"There's always more stupidity to be discovered in this tired old world," he said, and I believed he was about to puke over the side.

"My parents aren't stupid. You can't swim, you stay with your boat and have a better chance of being sighted and saved."

"You afraid of sinking?" he asked and pushed back his hair. Water dripped off his chin.

"Not on the water but in it I'd be."

"You're a goddamn curiosity."

"Reckon you could teach me to swim?"

"Rocks don't float," he said.

Mama's legs had grown thick at her ankles. All the standing she did working at Morgan's Seafood. She came home tired and dropped into a chair, which is why I did most the cooking. I hoped my legs wouldn't settle like hers when I grew older, but knew that was likely. What you'd call a fat chance.

"We needing bread?" she asked while I baked. She'd toed off her shoes and rolled down her stockings. She sighed lots. I understood what she really meant by the question.

"William's father asked me to keep an eye on him," I said.

"All kinds of eyes," she said.

"I wish people in this family would just leave me to my knitting," I said.

"It's not knitting I'm thinking about," she said. "It's what the knitting might end up being used for."

"I'm never discussing the subject ever again," I said and leaving slammed the screen door so hard my dough fell.

William was drinking less and swimming more. I phoned his father collect and told him.

"He led the team at Washington and Lee," Mr. Cabell said. "It's a good sign."

I wouldn't accept any money from Mr. Cabell, but he had Lands' End mail me a teal-green shirt. I wore it over to William's, though I'd never tell him where it came from. He didn't notice anyhow.

I kept after him to teach me to swim. From Sears I ordered a rose-colored bathing suit that had a little ruffled skirt to cover the tops of my heavy thighs. I didn't really expect him to give in, but on a July evening when air seared the skin and locusts seemed to be screeching all over the universe, he pushed up from his chair.

"Let's douse the heat," he said. He went in the cottage and came back wearing cut-off jeans and a soiled T-shirt. I tried not to look at the scars on his legs.

I rode him over to the house where I pulled on my bathing suit. I felt nervous and naked in it, but he hardly glanced at me. Off our dock was a mud bottom, so I carried him to a sandy cove at the south entrance to the inlet and beached the skiff.

He walked out hip deep and arched under the water. I waded to my waist and dodged a nettle idly pumping with the tide and streaming tentacles.

"You got to give yourself to it," William said. "Don't fight. Let the water take hold of you and relax."

"Get my hair wet."

"Terrific loss. Still there's a chance the world might survive."

I pushed forward and could stretch out only a second before I sank. Coughing and blowing, I gathered my feet 'neath me.

"Hopeless," he said and swam out into the channel, charted at twenty feet. He looked so fine and easy belonging to the water I felt shamed.

I shut my eyes and made myself push off a second time. All right, I thought, I'll drown if I have to. I sank and saw a sook lying dead on the shadowy bottom. My body began to rise. At least the front half did. My legs dragged.

Trouble was I coasted over a steep drop-off. The water

turned dark under me. I began to flail. I glimpsed William circling 'round me to the skiff. Oh God, I thought, he's going to let me die.

He held an oar to me. I clutched it, and he pulled me to shallows where I could stand. I'd swallowed a gallon of salty water. This time I thought I might be the one to puke.

"You'll never make the Olympic team," he said.

"You coulda reached me a hand," I said as I slogged to the skiff and held the transom to support myself.

"Oh, yeah," he said. "Right."

I kept my distance from William, yet meant to learn to swim. Afternoons when I finished pulling pots, I beached the skiff at the cove. I worked at floating and paddling ten feet at a time, not out in the deep part but paralleling the shoreline. After I could do ten, I worked on twenty. I marked distances by using my big toe to scratch stripes in sand. I practiced holding my breath even home in bed. I got so I could halfway give myself to the water, though I wasn't near developing a college-boy stroke like William but just sort of flippered along with my head high, my legs still dragging.

I hadn't crossed a deep spot. I needed to do that 'fore I could really call myself a swimmer. I moved out a little farther in the channel. Finally I got nerve enough to swim out to day marker 8, about twenty yards offshore. I held on to the pile to catch my breath, careful not to get slashed by barnacles, and then made it back to the beach. I hooted and danced around like a wild Indian.

I was ready to brag to William. Been a while since I took him food. I fixed myself up a little. I'd ordered a blue cotton dress from Sears, the only girdle I ever owned in my entire life, a pair of dawn-colored nylons, and no high heels but a pair of white slings.

Also got a perm at the Heavenly Hair Haven. I borrowed Mama's angel-shell necklace and two costume rings as well as stoppered on Navy Cover Girl perfume and stood close to the bathroom mirror to apply lipstick. Glad nobody was home to make remarks.

I drove my Lariat over Saturday afternoon. Should've turned right around and gone back. William sat drinking on the deck. His khakis were filthy, and he could've used a sheep shearing. If he even looked at me I couldn't tell because of those damn sunglasses. He didn't speak but let me stand there feeling the fool.

"An announcement," I said. "I'm now a genuine swimmer."

"Ah," he said and raised a Dixie cup to his mouth. The vodka bottle he'd set between his bare feet. Did "Ah" mean he believed me, was pleased, or what? His was the only chair. I waited feeling more stupid by the second. A plane flew over. Though I shaded my eyes, I couldn't find it in the sky's shattery brightness.

"Always wanted to fly," I said.

"It's not the flying but the landings."

"Guess being a pilot you'd know," I said and soon as the words left my mouth realized I'd spoke wrong.

"How'd you find out I was a pilot?"

"Heard folks at Port Haven mention it," I said, and my eyes slipped sideways. I never could lie good.

"People in Port Haven don't know," he said. "You been talking to somebody."

"Your father," I said. I was willing to carry even a well-meant lie only so far 'cause you could get even more tangled up if you kept going. "What you got against loving parents who're grieving for you?"

"What I got is they taught me a beautiful backhand, how to eat an avocado, the way to set the jib, but never warned me about Dr. Gravitas," he said and had himself a big swallow of vodka.

"Who's Dr. Gravitas?"

"A comical looking little man. He wears a derby and carries a furled umbrella and leather satchel. He has on granny glasses, sports a trimmed black mustache, and just when you think you're flying high he reaches up with the crook of that umbrella, pulls you down to earth, and opens the satchel. What he lifts out is shit."

"That's crazy liquor talk," I said. "Your parents good people who care for you."

"What do you know?" he asked and emptied the Dixie cup. As he struggled to work his way out of the chair, he tilted. I reached to right him. He flinched like my fingers were fire.

"Afraid some woman'll touch you?" I asked.

"What woman? You see any women around here?"

"Whatever did I do to you that'd cause you to say such a mean hurting thing to me?" I said and stepped away.

I drove off and waited till I was hidden by a myrtle thicket before I cried.

I got home before my parents. I hid away my new finery. I'd picked up the boxes at the post office, and nobody knew what all I'd bought.

One last thing I meant to show William. He'd find I could swim if he never learned another thing about me.

Sunday I didn't drive to church with Mama and Daddy. I told them I wasn't feeling too sprightly, a truth. Soon as they left, I looked through my nocs to spot William on his deck.

I changed into my bathing suit, motored the skiff across the harbor, and killed the Evinrude in front of his cottage. He wore the sunglasses, so I couldn't tell if he was watching me or not.

I lowered myself over the side, worked my hands along the gunnel to the bow to get situated, and let go. I glimpsed him stand and cross to the deck railing. I meant to swim just once all the way around the skiff. That done, I'd climb aboard and run home never to see William again if I could help it.

A northwest breeze feathered the water. The skiff began to drift. I should've tossed over the anchor. I paddled toward her, but she slowly moved off. I swam harder. Still the gap increased as she glided away as if under sail.

Don't panic, I ordered myself, and gained on the skiff till I ran face first into nettles floating in on the tide. I tried to circle them but felt their stingings along my chest, thighs, and legs. The skiff drifted farther.

I thought of turning and reaching shore off William's cottage. He definitely stood watching. No, sir, I'd not let him see me losing the skiff and become an even bigger idiot in his eyes.

Nettles everywhere. A convention. They slimed my legs and arms, dragged at my body, and the stinging went from hurt to pain. I was tiring but again cut the stretch of water between me and the skiff. Then I couldn't seem to draw closer, like she was a pet teasing me.

I treaded water and watched her widen the distance. My arms lost strength. At last giving myself to the water felt easy. I was up to my chin, yet burning all over.

I slipped under, kicked up, sank. All around nettles floated, moonylike gauzy parachutes pulsing in the grainy water, dangling misty ornaments on a sea tree. A red devil floated by so beautiful I tried to pick it. Tentacles flowed among my fingers like strands of a tearing silk scarf.

I looked down to the bottom darkness and lo and behold saw Dr. Gravitas. Sure enough the hook of his umbrella rose to me, yet everything felt warm and lazy, the ornaments hanging so pretty, and me too just curling along with the sleepy pull of the tide.

Till another kind of pulling and then scraping along my body and through shifting gray light the dim shape of a phantom that wasn't Dr. Gravitas at all but William's face drawing away. His sunglasses were gone, and he dripped on me. Best I could make out, I lay sprawled in mud among reeds as he bent to me, pinched my nose, and laid his mouth over mine.

I choked coughing and closed my eyes. I felt his hands stripping away nettles. "Live," he said. "Goddamnit, don't you die on me."

Burning gave way to the cooling touches and swipes of his fingers. No dying. He again breathed hisself— *himself*—into me.

TENANT

Dexter emerged as I jammed the posthole digger into soil that an early summer drought had cooked into hardened, nearly impenetrable clay. Each time the blades struck the ground they sent painful jolts up through the wooden handles to my arms and shoulders. My head ached, I thirsted, flies spiraled about my stinging sweat, and I felt dizzy despite numerous salt tablets.

I labored at putting in a barbed-wire fence bordering a stand of Virginia shortleaf pines along the western boundary of my property. Dexter apparently had slipped from shadows and stood for a time watching me before revealing himself.

"Spring not fifty feet from here," he said, a slow, soft voice from the angular, unshaved face of a thin, long-legged man. Despite the heat, he wore a gray fedora set level, a white shirt buttoned at the collar, and a dark blue suit that gave off a metallic luster—wrinkled, dusty, baggy at the knees and elbows.

"What you want is dig your holes a foot deep, fill 'em with water, and wait till they soften. Beat yourself to death way you going at it."

"Didn't know about any spring," I said. Government expert that I was, I hadn't thought about anything as simple as filling the holes with water. I hailed from Toledo, Ohio, and had been working as a legislative assistant to the Honorable George L. Scanlon, congressman from my home state. Old George had lost his seat to a young firebrand Republican, costing me my D.C. job.

"Name's Barlow," the man said and extended a narrow, bony hand. "Dexter Barlow."

"Jeffrey Cole," I said, shook his hand, and felt the curbed strength of his grip. His horny fingernails wanted paring but no dirt rimmed them.

"Show you that spring," he said.

Distrustful and reluctant—did he mean to rob me?—I laid the posthole digger on the ground and followed into the pine woods. Parched needles crackled under my L. L. Bean boots, yet also felt spongy. The land sloped to a bowl-shaped wooded depression and a quiet pool of darkened water.

Beside it a Campbell's tomato soup can had been upended on a broken bough stuck in moist ground. Water oozed and dripped from mossy imbedded shale into the pool, sending shivers across the surface.

"Sweet and never knowed her to run dry," Dexter said, dipped the can, and offered it to me.

I hesitated because the soup can was rusting and didn't appear exactly hygienic. Moreover deer, coon, and other wild animals roamed these woods. Their droppings could pollute the water. At my hesitation, Dexter withdrew the can to drink fully from it. His blondish hair needed cutting and swung away from his ears and neck as his chin lifted. He again filled the can and presented it to me.

"Not thirsty," I said, though my scratchy throat felt clogged.

He turned his face sideways to look at me from corners

of eyes bluish gray, direct and startlingly unsullied in his sun-browned face. A smile twitched his mouth.

"Appears you could use help planting your fence," he said and upended the can on the bough. "Two dollars a hole and I'll dig 'em three feet deep and tamp in the posts."

I swiped at biting deer flies. Blisters that had burst despite my work gloves stung my hands. I suffered from allergies that brought on itching, rashes, and sneezing. Furthermore I felt harassed and discouraged because cutworms had chewed down half the tomato plants, rabbits had gnawed the lettuce, and crows plucked up sweet corn almost as fast as it sprouted.

"Give you a try," I said.

"Need a bucket," he said.

He walked beside me to the two-story house that had four large bedrooms, a dog trot, a side porch, and lightning rods shaped like arrows that pointed from the tin roof at the sky. Red oak shade only partially cooled the parched lawn.

The property had been owned by an aging farmer who let things slide. At his death a Tobaccoton bank put the place the market. I saw an ad in the *Post*—seventy acres and the house offered at $110,000. Carol and I drove down to Southside Virginia from Chevy Chase. I counteroffered $100,000 and our bid was accepted. We wondered whether we'd been taken.

We'd owned a brick rancher we got $198,000 for, bought the farm, and believed we had plenty left over to refurbish our purchase. City born and bred, I'd always wanted to work land, grow all the food set on my table, and become as self-sufficient as possible in a suffocatingly complex world.

"Christ, you don't know any more about farming than I

do," Carol had said. She hailed from New Haven, had attended Mount Holyoke, and specialized in ornithological research for the Smithsonian. "I've never planted even a potato."

"We can do it," I'd said. "Live cheap, and it'll give us time to finish our book."

Evenings worn and exhausted from work and D.C. traffic, we'd fixed drinks and talked of writing a suspense novel that involved the placing of a sexually compromised legislative assistant on the staff of the Senate majority leader with the intent both of supplying information to the Japanese Ministry of Trade and influencing legislation useful to the Land of the Rising Sun.

Carol had published short stories in several literary quarterlies, and our novel would depend greatly on her writing skills and my insider's knowledge of the government's workings.

We'd been prompted by another reason for changing the pattern of our lives. Over recent years our marriage had sprung a slow leak. We'd not been unfaithful, sulked, or battled. After an initial passion, our days had settled to a ho-hum workday routine that had all the enchantment of a trip across an arid plain, no water hole in sight. We'd hoped for a renewal of spirit, a rebuilding of our lives together, and had taken the leap to buy the farm.

Our first night the early April weather turned wet and cold, the house had no central heating, and the electricity had not been reconnected as promised. When I built a fire in the downstairs bedroom, the chimney wouldn't draw. We bumped around among unopened bags, boxes, and crates as I coughed and raised windows.

"Where are my city lights?" Carol cried, her arms spread

dramatically. She lit candles, and in their wavering light a fallen lick of dark hair across her pale forehead appeared a wound.

God, the labor we drove ourselves to—she inside stripping wallpaper, removing paint from mantels and stair rails, sanding, varnishing, while I scraped and painted the house's dry wood siding, replaced and puttied broken window panes, and fixed leaks in the roof.

I learned to drive the secondhand Ford tractor to bushhog fields grown entangled with briars, thistles, and thorny honey locust trees. I plowed a garden plot which, after consulting the county agent, I fertilized and limed. I started the fence to hold the cattle we planned to buy.

Not only the labor but the flaying heat of southside Virginia bled our energy. The house lacked air conditioning. We rose at first light to work during the morning coolness, but by noon we sagged and moved about listless and hollow-eyed.

Carol still had to hang curtains, and we'd yet to bleach and refinish the aged and begrimed pine floors. Completing my fence line seemed an endless project. Neither she nor I spoke the words we knew dwelt in the other's mind: *This has all been a sonofabitch of a mistake.*

At the house I found Dexter a bucket. When Carol walked out on the back porch and I introduced them, his lifting of his gray fedora was more than just the removal of a hat—a half sweep of the arm close to a cavalier gesture.

"Pleasing to have good people in the neighborhood," Dexter said and didn't reset his hat till he took the bucket from me and turned away toward the field and unfinished fence.

"Has a certain gallant air," Carol said, a smudge on her cheek. She wore tennis shoes, paint-splattered khaki shorts and shirt, and a red bandanna tied around her head. "And spooky eyes."

Dexter hung his jacket on a fencepost and worked without a break the rest of the afternoon. I checked on him from the roof, which I patched with steel shingles found in our mildewed basement. At five o'clock I crossed the field to him as he used my iron tamping bar to set a locust post. Together we fitted in cedar rails. He'd finished nine sections—at least double the rate I'd have completed in a like amount of time.

"Ready to quit?" I asked.

"Okay with you, I'll keep at her till dark."

"You're not eating?"

"Got food," he said.

Maybe he'd stashed a sack holding a sandwich or can of beans among the pines. Because of the spring, he wouldn't need a soda. I told him to come to the house when he wanted his pay.

At dusk he knocked on the back door. For me he didn't remove his hat. He'd done five more sections. As I paid, he asked for another day's work. I agreed and watched him move off toward the woods, his shape merging into seeping darkness.

Next morning when I stood at the window to dress, I looked across the field. The orchard grass glimmered from dew the red half-risen sun had not yet burned off. Dexter worked at the fence.

"Chances are we've found ourselves a good man," I said.

"If we ever again take a vacation, I intend to do nothing but sleep," Carol said. She stretched and groaned.

" 'Go to the ant, thou sluggard.' "

"You just plain go to hell, you two-faced hypocrite."

"All hypocrites are two-faced," I said.

"You want war in this family, just keep on the way you're going," she said.

While I nailed shingles on the roof, I watched Dexter carry buckets of water from the spring, pour, and dig. At noon he glanced at the sun and when he walked into the woods didn't immediately return. I'd been timing him. I assumed he was resting or eating. He stayed fourteen minutes.

That evening he took his pay and asked could he rent the one-story tenant house at the rear of the property. It'd not been lived in for years—broken windows gaped, the floor felt mushy, a hornets' nest hung menacingly from an exposed rough-hewn ceiling beam, wind and sun had honed off most paint, and the plank siding had bowed and weathered a pearly gray.

"Fix her up for you if you let me bunk there," he said.

"No water or plumbing."

"There's a pitcher pump I can repair and a privy."

I said I'd have to talk to Carol, and he left. She reared from all fours where she'd been using steel wool on the heart-of-pine boards of our parlor.

"Where's he living now?" she asked.

"Didn't think to inquire. He's polite, a steady worker, the price is right, and we need him bad."

"He must be poor, always wears that cheap suit he somehow keeps halfway neat. Dirt doesn't seem to stick to him."

I gave Dexter permission to move into the tenant house, rent eight dollars a week to be withheld from wages.

The house had never been wired. We'd see the light

of his kerosene lamp flicker across the pasture and hear hammering far into the night. He sprayed the hornets, reinforced the floor, swept and scrubbed, installed windowpanes, rehung a door. The rusty squeak of the pitcher pump brought up water at first discolored brown but finally splashed clear. He borrowed and returned my tools.

"See any furniture?" Carol asked.

I hadn't, and Sunday afternoon I walked the path to the house. Dexter had scythed the weeds around it. He sat on the wooden steps he'd rebuilt. Shirtless and shoeless, he held a long-blade, bone-handled clasp knife and peeled a red apple.

I attempted to sneak looks past him into the house without being obvious but glimpsed only bare newly installed plasterboard that ran straight through to the back door. What southerners called a shotgun house and did he own even a table and chair? Sunlight glazed his bony feet.

"Got a pair of Levi's that never fit right," I said, a lie Carol had put me up to. "You're welcome to them."

"Reckon I'm okay now in the clothes department," he said, using the knife precisely, the apple peeling spiraling down lazily off the blade's glinting sharpness as if of its own will.

He'd bought himself work shoes, coveralls, and a green billed cap.

"Too proud to accept charity," Carol said as she wiggled into a yellow summer dress before driving to Tobaccoton's new Food Lion. She stopped at the Little Ritz Hair Salon for a trim and shampoo. When she returned, she told me the owner was a woman named Windy Belle.

"These damn southern names," I said.

"Quaint huh?"

"Oh for sure."

"Windy Belle brought up Dexter," Carol said. "Pumped me for information. Finally mentioned he'd been in prison. Killed a man in a tonk fight. Recently paroled and living, Windy Belle claims, in an abandoned tobacco barn till we rented him the tenant house. Windy Belle says he's a wild man, especially when drinking."

"You're thinking we ought to run him off?"

"The news is more than a trifle unsettling."

"He's fixed up the tenant house. Painted it inside and out. He can repair anything around the place and offered to help me stock cattle."

"But we don't know him really. Might be best to tell him we can't afford him any longer."

"I'll do it tomorrow," I said.

That night I lay thinking of Dexter out there alone in the tenant house surrounded by darkness into which the kerosene lamp splayed a flickering unearthly light. Fury might still burn in him, and he could be watching and waiting for an opportunity to rob us or worse.

Midmorning I found him at his garden plot. He hunkered beside a row of what the locals called snaps, picking the newly ripened elongated pods and dropping them into the galvanized bucket he used at the fence.

He hadn't heard me approach, and what struck me was the gentleness of his hands as I stood watching, the long fingers not unfeelingly tearing the string beans from the bushes but detaching them as if showing deference and regret at the violation.

As a young buck a drunken passion might've ignited him to a riotous act, but no fury burned in this garden.

When he noticed me, I asked about blackened lengths of hemp rope lying among the rows.

"Crows and other birds scared of snakes," he said. "Keeps them out. You know we could get us a late hay cutting off the front field, store bales till winter, and sell them. Somebody always needs hay. And here, take these snaps. Already got more inside than I can swaller."

How could I lay him off when he was so amiable and I'd witnessed what I judged to be the inner tenderness of the man? At the house where Carol waited, I held the bucket to her.

"His fingers?" she asked. "You backed off because of his fingers on green beans?"

"Let's take a chance and give him a little more time. He just might turn this place into a paying farm."

"I admit I like his style but tender fingers," Carol said and rattled out a pot to cook up the snaps we ate two nights running.

Dexter and I mowed hay. He suggested I run the tractor in third gear at half throttle, make a reverse cut around the outer edge of the field before beginning decreasing circles in the other direction to lay the rest of the orchard grass on the ground, and back the Ford and use the hydraulic lift to flap the blade when the mower's clattering teeth clogged up.

We loaded bales on the wagon and hauled them to the barn as well as heaved and slung them into the loft where we stacked them in spaced rows that allowed ventilation gaps for curing.

"They don't dry right, they get moldy or too hot," he explained. "Barns has caught fire."

We worked shirtless. Palls of chaff covered our sweaty

skins. Mine became nearly as brown as his, not a beach tan, but the coarser sort, the badge of honest redneck labor. I felt the good ache of sore muscles honorably earned and a headiness from a job accomplished.

A mile and eight-tenths down the road from our farm at Jericho Crossroads stood a general store known as Wimpy's, though no sign identified it. I bought fuel at one of the two Crown pumps. Evenings local sons of the soil gathered to sit on a split-log bench and swap stories.

Wimpy was a shrunken, hairless ancient who seemed without eyelids, and when he blinked, the act itself startled. As I left after paying him, a bearded man on the bench rose to follow me. His Big Boy overalls fit loosely over a sleeveless undershirt. I smelled the scent of chewing tobacco, which bulged his jaw and moistly stained corners of his mouth. He reset his John Deere cap.

"Dexter still out your way?" he asked and worked that chaw with shoves of his tongue.

"Yes, sir, he is."

"Killed my half brother over a flame-haired gal named Windy Belle," he said and spat to the side, causing dust to spume. "Cut him belly button to chin. Oughten to be caged up."

Windy Belle. There couldn't be more than one even in Tobaccoton, could there? I asked, "Do you mean the hair dresser at the Little Ritz?"

"The same," he said.

"Hasn't Dexter paid his debt for that?"

"Some debts never gets paid," he said, spat a second time, and turned to amble heavily back to the porch where men rooted to the bench watched the empty road before them.

At the house I told Carol about Windy Belle.

"I suspected she was interested in more than just routine gossip," Carol said. "Can't go in there she doesn't work around to changing the subject to Dexter."

"She a flame-haired sexpot?"

"Maybe once. Still has the hair, but she's plump, wears too much makeup, butchers the language. So she got herself a man killed over her."

"You sound like she carried home a trophy."

"Dexter had to love deeply to slay for her."

"That makes it right?"

"It's horrible and brutish, but she's got to wonder at how much he cared, the power of his love for her. Terrible as the knifing was, won't she forever marvel at the thought, 'He did it all for me,' a perverse but highest kind of adoration?"

Dexter helped purchase a dozen Black Angus steers. We drove to the Tobaccoton stockyard and sat on wooden bleacher seats around the manure-snarled sawdust of the auction ring. He nudged me when to bid.

"Go high or low," he advised. "Buy either scrubs or the best. No money in the middle."

We trucked the steers to the farm. Carol and I liked seeing them settle in, nose the fences, and graze across pasture. They gave meaning to the place, made it real and not just a playground of two city slickers with more dollars than sense.

Late October delivered the first kill frost followed by a balmy Indian summer that brought a lassitude to the land and to us. Since Dexter'd taken over more of the work, Carol and I slept later. We hated getting up in darkness.

At a weekly Friday shopping trip to Food Lion, she whispered to me the words "Windy Belle."

The woman stood holding a head of cabbage before the vegetable bin. She wore red wedgies, white socks, red slacks, and a pleated white shirt fronted with large red buttons. She smiled at Carol, who introduced me.

Windy Belle was definitely no beauty—powdered, rouged, the makings of a double chin, weight settled into her hips, but a lively face and the long flaming hair braided into pigtails swung forward over her shoulders.

She and Carol complained about the price of lettuce. Carol wanted a permanent and promised to phone for an appointment.

"The great thing about perms is they not," Windy Belle said and laughed loudly, her painted lips opened wide.

Carol and I carried our groceries to the white Dodge Ram 4×4 we'd traded for our blue Honda. Tobaccoton was pickup city, and we tried to make ourselves part of it, though our accents never fooled natives.

"He did it over her?" I asked as we pulled away.

"If you look hard, you can see the ghost of a young, shapely, vivacious girl able to drive men wild. And I saw you taking in her knockers."

"A scientific observation noted in an attempt to understand events of the past."

"Tit statistics," Carol said.

The steers fattened and grew sleek, the apple trees had been pruned, the fencing stood stout and impenetrable. Sure enough, somebody wanted the late cutting of hay and paid $2.00 a bale, half of which I turned over to Dexter for his work—the total $190.00.

Cold blew in bringing gritty snow. Carol and I took two hours each morning for work on the novel. We set legal tablets and our computer on the dining-room table. I blocked out a big sex scene between the suave, mustached spy and the senator's stylish wife, a romp we believed obligatory for marketability. Carol dressed it in her silky prose.

"You never tried any of these fancy moves on me," she said.

"It's a book," I said.

"But operating in your mind."

"You're always in my mind."

"Me and the price of beef."

We made occasional love, no searing passion, yet each cordial and competent in the bed. Several of our Chevy Chase friends had divorced, and one couple had thrown a party to celebrate their breakup. Despite our lack of highs, Carol and I believed we'd succeeded in working our marriage through to a mature and enduring partnership.

As to the price of beef, Dexter suggested we might let our Angus go.

"Cattle prices rising because of what blizzards done out west," he said. "Our herd's put on weight, and you won't need to feed the rest of winter."

We collected a $1,700 profit on the sale. When I wafted the livestock market check before Carol's face, she snatched it from my hand, and that night we celebrated with too much Chablis and sank to sleep talking of the novel—in our vinous condition the sale and success of which seemed as sure as the sunrise.

I woke believing the sound I heard was the wind blowing from the west and fluting over chimney tops as well as fluttering our weather striping. I slipped from bed to cross to the bathroom, where I pushed aside the curtain. A full moon silvered the oaks, the wheat-stubbled field, the tenant house where I glimpsed a moving shape.

I tiptoed downstairs and out the kitchen door to the cold, blustery porch. A man ran in circles around the tenant house, arms spread, his shadow cast ahead, to the side, behind. He stopped, raised his face to the moon, and cried as if suffering unbearable pain.

Dexter. I started to hurry to him but remembered what I'd heard of his past drinking and wildness. I thought *knife.*

I stepped back quick and bolted the door. Through the kitchen window I watched him spin twice, howl at the sky, and move off in a clumsy, zigzagging course to enter the tenant house where the kerosene lamp burned, its glow nearly enveloped by moonlight.

I climbed the stairs and settled beside Carol. She mumbled but didn't rouse. I couldn't sleep and in the morning said nothing about what I'd seen. I fixed coffee, carried her a mug, and went to find Dexter.

I located him in the equipment shed greasing the tractor's wheel bearings. I couldn't see that his carousing had marked him.

"Hear a fuss around here last night?" I asked.

From the bearing's nipple he withdrew the lubricant gun and looked up without answering.

"Sounded like somebody living high," I said.

"You thinking me?" he asked, those blue-gray eyes fastened on mine with a stare that did not give. A second time I thought *knife*—the bone-handled one he carried. I pictured the apple peeling spiraling effortlessly from the blade.

"Dexter, your word's good around here," I said, backing

off, yet troubled. He hadn't denied it'd been him. I didn't tell Carol and worried what might happen if he'd gone back to the bottle.

Saturday Carol and I drove to Lynchburg to blow a portion of our new money so well earned it had to spend better. She bought a wool skirt and I a pair of rubber boots and fur-lined gloves. We lunched at Emil's, allowing ourselves two-olive martinis before ordering shrimp cocktails and broccoli quiche.

Monday I expected Dexter to be at the shed continuing to perform maintenance on machinery we'd need in early spring. He didn't show. I waited thirty minutes before walking to the tenant house and tapping on his door. No answer. I called his name as I opened the door and looked into emptiness.

I didn't want him to think I was snooping and felt anxious as I walked through. No chair, no table, no bed. All kitchen utensils and clothing taken. Nothing left except the galvanized bucket and a broom, the bristles worn short to the binding.

"Just gone?" Carol asked and her palms dropped against her Levi's.

"Everything's clean. Not a speck of dust. Eat off the floor."

"Why run out on us without a word?"

"Maybe a better offer."

"I can't believe he'd not tell us good-bye after the way we've treated him. What we get for having faith in a redneck ingrate."

"He could've had troubles we don't know about."

"Who doesn't?" she asked.

•   •   •

We read about it in the Lynchburg *News & Advance* delivered each morning by a man named Snipes who drove a pickup to the box at the head of our lane—the discovery of the two bodies on a grassy strip of bank along the Appomattox River. I carried the paper to Carol. She stared at me.

Windy Belle had been strangled and laid out, her arms at her sides, her eyes closed. Dexter apparently positioned himself beside her before slicing both wrists.

"Jesus," Carol said, all shaky. "How could anybody do such a thing?"

We read the newspaper notice about Windy Belle's funeral to be held at the Healing Spring Baptist Church. Carol and I talked about attending but didn't, uncertain what people would think of us for having hired Dexter. No information given about his burial.

The sheriff drove out to talk to us and look at the tenant house. He was a portly man but not soft or fat, his face drawn taut over a prominent jawline, his hair bronze-colored, his uniform neatly pressed. He leveled his tan trooper's hat.

"No funeral for Dexter," he said. "Nobody wanted him. Sent his corpse down to Richmond's med school. People 'round Tobaccoton loved Windy Belle. A hundred at graveside."

"Still can't believe it," Carol said.

"They had them a hot fire burning a long time ago, but she gone past him over the years, yeah, gone past him. Dexter kept coming back at her, wouldn't turn loose. Drove him crazy she'd have no part of him. Took her as she was leaving the Little Ritz and carried her down to the river cove where they'd once courted. Before you saw all the blood, you'd thought they was just lying there enjoying a sunny day."

We moved numbly through the rest of the afternoon and went to bed early to stay warm—a still, cold night. I woke, and Carol no longer lay beside me. I found her standing at the bathroom window.

She gazed across the frozen field. The waning moon spread a pale, icy luminescence that reflected off panes of glass, causing the tenant house to appear eerily lighted from within as if by Dexter's kerosene lamp.

"Enough," I said and fumbled for her hand. I worked my fingers among her passive ones and stepped back to draw her from the window and the cold light that entranced her.

During days that followed we mostly avoided looking toward the tenant house, tried to reserve a space in our vision like a black hole to contain it. Yet through the spring and summer we couldn't avoid seeing weeds grow and claim Dexter's garden. Poison oak snaked up prying hairy passages among plank siding. A blue jay flew into a windowpane, breaking the glass and falling dead.

"Let's get rid of the damn thing," Carol said. She invited the Tobaccoton Fire Department to burn the tenant house. The trucks drove out with sirens shrilling, and veteran members struck matches but allowed green volunteers to extinguish the blaze.

We watched dirty brown smoke twist upward among licking red flames. Hoses arched water from the pumper truck. The smoke bent away and spread over pines bordering the field. Pulsing embers glowed through the night. The smell of charred wood and ashes lingered for weeks.

We struggled to finish the book, named it *Dark Moon of*

the Rising Sun, spent seemingly endless packaging and postage costs, but found no publisher. Our fifth year we sold the farm at a $24,000 profit to a young couple from New York State who planned to raise sheep. I'd not been able to hire dependable help, and the unremitting toil and a dwindling income bled the last romance from my dreams of self-sufficiency.

I applied for and was hired for a staff job with Kentucky's Senator Buster Crowe. Carol and I put our farm money down on a two-room townhouse in Silver Spring, Maryland, previously occupied by a bachelor astronomer who worked for NASA.

Carol arranged a return to the Smithsonian. In a few short months our lives sank back into the same frantic, life-draining routine we'd struggled to escape, and we'd feel we had never left the District.

Frequently the city's sirens invaded our walls. For days they caused momentary stases, a meeting of eyes, and gazes into distances beyond our rooms' confinements, resurrecting memories that whispered around us like cold drafts from the heart.

WINTER WHEAT

I tend my rows. The earth knows me, and I the earth. The plow points curl waves of red soil. An ocean of earth and as big a bitch as any sea. I am the forgiver.

A river of seed drilled behind the disk harrow. Appears I'm never fully paid up on nitrogen and pesticides. The labor causes my eyes to haze and sweat to find every crease of my field-seasoned body. A salty drop falls on an escaping black ant, and it hustles away in twisting crippled fashion. What lies does it tell the nest?

I first see Jessie Hamlett, a tiny doll-faced woman, at Mount Laurel Church. It is early April. She's come to fill in for Rebecca Goode, our regular piano player, who's down with back misery. Jessie isn't from Red Oak but Tobaccoton where she teaches third grade at the Howell County Consolidated School.

I don't speak to her at the Sunday service. Preacher Walmsley announces her name and thanks her for helping. I don't snoop to uncover her address either. Tobaccoton's a small, flat, sun-baked town. I'll find out without anybody at Mount Laurel knowing.

I drive my F-150 to Tobaccoton the next Saturday morning. I have removed tools, hosed off the truck, and swept the cab. I wear my go-to-meeting dark suit, white shirt, and brown tie. First thing I do when I reach town is stop by Southern States Co-op where dust from the roaring hammermill spins 'round the loading dock like yellow bees and dims a broken sunlight.

I pay my feed bill and borrow the phone book. Jessie Lacy Hamlett's name is on the page. Her address, 904-A River Street. I don't need to ask the whereabouts of River Street and drive till I spot the white gabled house that has a wrap-around porch. There are two front screen doors. I squint. The left door is A.

I park in a curb strip of elm shade, get set comfortable, and wait. I see her shape cross a second-story window. The sill box is planted with red-blooming geraniums. She reaches out a long-spout watering can.

She leaves the house early afternoon wearing a tan skirt and pink blouse. Her limp isn't bad noticeable. Just a little tug to the left every other step. She has a quick, busy walk. She palms her hands up under her glossy black hair to cool the rear of her neck.

I follow downtown to Main where she stops at a store named the Fashion Feast. She stays inside twenty-seven minutes. She is trying on clothes. When she leaves, she carries a blue plastic shopping bag that flashes sunlight.

She crosses to the Tobaccoton Mercantile, which has bins filled with vegetables under the striped awning shadowing the sidewalk. She selects a baking potato, a broccoli head, and half a sack of English peas. Only a person living alone buys like that.

She is known and speaks to people. Her smile seems too big for such a face. She walks back along River Street, and I watch her walk into A and the screen door close.

I drive home. I work a garden behind the house left me by my daddy. He built it himself, sawing his own yellow pines, fashioning the cedar shakes, laying the checkered linoleum, and he and my mama lived in it near forty years before meeting the Lord face-to-face.

Me and my sister Bess are the only children. Bess graduated from a Danville business school and now works as a note teller at the Southside Bank in that city. We don't see much of each other. It embarrasses her that I smell of the barn and spit in front of her friends.

During the summer I slip into Tobaccoton with pickings from my garden—tomatoes, cucumbers, snaps, butterbeans, sweet corn—and at dark I sneak up to Miss Jessie's house, leave the sack in front of her door, and ring the bell. She hurries down the steps to answer it. By the time she reaches the door I've run across the yard and street to my pickup.

She catches me on a Friday. It's almost eleven, the mockingbird quieting, and her bedroom ceiling light has switched off. She tricks me by using her back door and stealing around to wait in the blacker night of a willow oak. She has set a lawn chair beside its trunk.

"You stop right there," she calls just as I'm straightening from leaving the sacks.

She walks out of darkness and shines a flashlight in my face. I take off my hat.

"Just who are you?" she asks. "And why you bringing me ten times more fresh vegetables than I can ever eat?"

"I saw you at Mount Laurel Church," I say.

"Don't remember you," she says.

"I sit in a back pew," I say.

"What reason you got for being so nice to me?" she asks.

"I like how you play the hymns," I say.

She laughs. The flashlight still aims at my face. What she

does is reach over and touch my arm as if she's been knowing me all her life.

"What's your name?" she asks.

And that's how we started.

I am big boned, my hands large, my feet heavy. Words
don't move easy from my mouth. I never finished school.
My nickname was Toad. I am slow but steady. After a hitch
in the navy, I took over the farm and have made it pay despite the drought years. Red dust clogged my snot, and I
felt hunger's midnight gnaw.

Truth is Miss Jessie don't have much chance except me.
That withered left calf of hers. She tries to hide it by wearing stockings, but a man really looking can't miss it. She,
like me, is laying on the years. When she don't know I'm
watching, I see lines of her face deepen. Powder don't cover
them.

I surprise her at the crab apple tree behind the apartment she rents. She stands bent and is staring at the
ground. She's been crying.

"The apples are so sour they bring tears," she says.

It wont apples but a man named Garland Fisher, who
ran a debit book for First Settlers. I saw them at the Howell County Fair whirling around in the Octopus. I heard
her screams. I could pick out her voice in a high wind.

Garland got a promotion that took him to Lynchburg.
Maybe she believed he'd come back. He didn't. She stops
watering the pansies that has replaced her geraniums in the
window box.

I ask her Christmas Eve. We've been to church, hers, the
Wesley Methodist where she plays. I bring a necklace I
made out of fairy stones collected from plowing. I bind

them in claws on loops of a silver chain, what'd been my mama's proudest jewelry piece. My daddy was a jackleg blacksmith who taught me fire and how to work metal. Silver's a hundred times easier than iron.

Miss Jessie has a little spruce Christmas tree I cut set on her dining table. I lay my present beside it. I wrapped it myself using a sheet of satiny red paper bought from the Dollar General. After she opens it, she stands looking at the necklace dangling across from her fingers.

"Fasten it on," she says, and I do. When she turns, I kiss her the best I know how. It's my first time with a woman.

I fix up the house for her—paint inside and out, a new bathroom, and a Sears electric dishwasher. I do most of the work, though she sews curtains and hangs the rosebud wallpaper she chose. She tacks up her framed college diploma and teaching certificate in the parlor. She wants bookcases, and I build her one out of a wild cherry tree a thunderstorm tipped over.

She asks for a telephone, a thing I've never seen the use of justify the cost, but no neighbors close, and she is social. I have Centel install an instrument downstairs. She entertains herself gossiping while I'm out the house. I tell her we don't need to spend money for long-distance when post cards will do.

She finds a job at the lower school in Red Oak. Her pay helps mightily when I lose a tobacco crop to hail after it does rain. She don't understand farming is half holding on till the good years. She becomes more grieved than me. She's been counting on buying rugs and a spinet piano. I give her a hundred-dollar bill from my secret roll in the

Clabber Girl baking soda can I keep taped tight and buried at the foot of my silo's concrete base.

Summers she works alongside me. We top and sucker tobacco, dose the plants, pull and rack the leaf. We tend the smoldering hickory needed for curing. She loves to read but she's too tired to turn a page during harvesttime.

Her parents is dead. She has a younger brother, Terry, who's an airline pilot down in Atlanta. He drives up to see her on her birthday. She's never told me how old she is. He takes her for a ride in his silver Thunderbird and has brought her a stereo set. He can't believe we don't have TV.

"Houses need music," Terry says, tall, curly headed, wearing an orange sport shirt, green slacks, and white slippers that you just slide feet into. A shoe of no worth around a farm.

"Work's our music," I say.

"Women like to dance," he says.

"We dance in the spirit," I say.

"Some step," he says.

Jessie loves and hugs him, but I am glad to see him go. He breaks the routine a man needs to finish his day's labor. I'm late drilling soybeans.

Jessie plays the stereo as she does housework. I hear snatches of music while in the field. She listens to a far distant Roanoke station. I can't understand the words they singing. Give me a fiddle and five-string banjo anytime.

I come home a night at dark after fixing a fence my bull has tore down trying to reach the heifers. I see her through the parlor window and believe somebody's visiting. She twirls, her arms held out like she has a partner, yet nobody else is in the house. Soon as I'm over the doorstep, she stops.

We almost have a child, six month's worth at the time she loses it. After her sickness, she don't much care to try for another. She stays up reading under her lamp. She asks me do I know of William Faulkner. I answer Billy Faulkner operates a planing saw at Tobaccoton's shook factory. I don't understand what's funny but smile to keep her happy.

The new principal at the Red Oak Lower School comes to services at Mount Laurel. He's fair skinned, got straw-colored hair, and looks like he's just been dipped and polished. Turns out to be a singer. He does "The Lord Has Risen" at Easter in a tenor voice that wobbles on high notes. The ladies coo around him and shake his soft hand, one that has never known a callus.

Jessie invites him to Sunday dinner. His name is Philip Sauers. "Call me Phil," he says. He eats only one wing of fried chicken, a dab of whipped potatoes, and a buttered biscuit, but passes his plate for seconds on a coconut cream pie Jessie has never served before. He hails from Charlottesville and holds his fork same as she does, which is different.

"I love the countryside, the people who work the land," he says.

"You ever work any land?" I ask and catch a look from Jessie.

"Not after your fashion," he says. "I did grow a dozen Big Boy tomatoes in the backyard of my parents' house."

As if growing a few 'maters is working land. What he don't know is the land she works you.

He's popular at the school, standing in the doorway greeting pupils, calling out and waving to everybody he meets at the Red Oak Market, seventeen miles down the road from the farm. The market is also the community post office. Acts like he's running for Congress.

He begins singing regular at Mount Laurel. Saturday afternoons he practices with Jessie. She drives over in the little Plymouth I bought her secondhand in Tobaccoton. She always takes a bath and changes clothes first.

"Seems to need lots of practice," I tell her when she gets home and scurries around to set dinner on the table by five.

"We're introducing new hymns," she says. "And he gives the church freely of his time, so I feel obliged to do the same."

"What's wrong with the old hymns?" I ask.

"Matthew, it livens people to try new things," she says. "Keeps us from growing old."

"Nothing keeps people from growing old," I say. "Except dying."

I'm not a jealous man. I do know myself to lack the open heartedness of others. What I'm best at is keep on keeping on. I don't believe feelings need to be put into words. A person might worship in the way he tends his rows. Love can be shown by what's brought to the table.

Jessie is taking better care of herself. She buys a yellow dress and matching pair of shoes that has black bows. Her dark stockings cover the withered calf. I smell perfume and see her sitting in the Plymouth using the rearview mirror while she paints on lipstick. She is giving herself to vanity.

On Friday ten days before school starts in September, she means to go down to Atlanta and help Terry celebrate his thirty-sixth birthday. She invites me along but has to know I can't break free with the corn harvest in full swing.

She bakes him a chocolate-covered angel food cake. I

carry it and her suitcase to the Plymouth. I watch her drive off down the lane between the ragged cedars. The dust she raises hangs instead of settling.

She has left spoon bread, collards, and slabs of our own salt-cured ham for my supper. In the dining room I eat while looking out the window to rows of tall corn stirred by a breeze. Another day of picking will bring in the last ears. Stalks to be cut for silage. I picture Jessie with pollen stuck to sweat of her face, a hand raised to shade eyes the same pretty blue as the copper sulphate I use to kill pond algae.

She believes I will never spend money to make a long-distance call. At nine-thirty I phone Terry. His number is written in a spiral notebook Jessie has kept from school. I find it in the second drawer of the dresser under her private garments.

"You like the cake?" I ask Terry.

"What cake?" he asks. "Got the matching belt and wallet that Jessie sent. She there?"

"No."

"Thank her for me."

"Don't get candle burnt," I say.

"What candles?"

I hang up.

She drives down the lane late Monday afternoon. I've had the phone taken out. I also hired Willie Garret to combine my soybeans, which ping like bullets into the bed of the GMC I run beside the gleaner. Good crop, likely thirty-five bushels to the acre.

She don't have dinner ready till six. She's tied on an apron over her housedress and wears no lip paint. I give the blessing. She won't look at me while I eat but keeps her eyes down and pokes at food, her fork held the proper way. When I finish and leave to return to the field, she sits waiting.

That night we lie on the oak bed my daddy built for my mama his bride. So heavy it takes two good men to lift. Jessie's restless beside me.

"You'll not speak to me?" she asks.

"You staying?" I answer.

"I'm too old for him," she says.

"You send a letter telling the school superintendent you got to quit teaching because of health reasons," I say. "Now I got a question for you."

"What?" she asks and is crying.

"Anybody eat that cake?" I ask.

She still thinks of him. I see it in the way she pauses about her work like she hears a voice when none is talking or in the soft way her fingers place and arrange wild daisies in a glass vase at the center of the table. She don't have a chance to talk to or see him but can't help holding on.

She and I quit speaking. She sets food before me, does the washing and chores, and nights instead of reading sews to keep her hands from fluttering like birds with no place to light. She's sleeping in the second bedroom.

She still plays the piano at Mount Laurel. Philip has stopped attending. A Saturday morning in early October she joins the Women of the Church for their annual conference at the Beautiful Plains Baptist in Danville. I see her and the other ladies off on the bus.

The evening stays hot, air moving up from the south and itching the skin. I drive the GMC to the Howell

County side of the river, park it in the pine woods, and hoof it to the moist black soil of the bank. Willow branches drag so lazily they hardly cause furrows in the water's flow. Yellow sycamore leaves drop to the quiet shaded surface and sail for a time.

Philip Sauers likes fishing and has himself an aluminum johnboat. He launches it off Hidden River's public landing and floats down to Miller's Bridge, which connects Randolph and Howell County.

I hunker and wait. The river is narrow and deep here, though downstream it widens and shallows. A blue twilight seems to rise from the water instead of lowering from the sky.

The johnboat rounds the bend and drifts beside the bank. Philip don't use a cane pole and worms but fishes with a fly rod. He's casting among low-hanging branches where bass or bream might be waiting for bugs to drop off.

He floats within twenty feet of me before he realizes I stand there. He's surprised and scared. He loses control of his line, which tangles around his reel.

"Lord, Matthew, for a second I thought you a bear," he says and lowers his rod to grab at the paddle.

"How's fishing?" I ask.

"Got a few suckers and a keeper smallmouth," he says, moving away with a swipe of the paddle. "What you doing here?"

"Truck broke down and need a ride to the bridge," I say.

"How come your truck's this side of the river?" he asks and uses the paddle to slow his drift.

"Loading billets," I say.

He hesitates turning toward shore. I step long and quick

into the johnboat, which gives under my weight. Water sluices over the side till I balance myself and sit facing him. He backs us from the bank.

"You fish?" he asks, his pale gray eyes darting about like mice running for cover in the corncrib.

"Been known to wet a line," I say and listen for others who might be on the river. A heron squawks, a frog bewhomps, and lightning bugs fire up beneath darkening sycamores.

"A man needs recreation," he says. "Get his mind off troubles of this old world."

"Same world, same troubles," I say.

"The living truth," he says and lowers the paddle to pick up the rod, untangle the line, and cast. A bream makes a pass at his yellow-and-green bug, which he pops from the water, a sound like a cork being pulled from a bottle. He's lost the fish 'fore it can hook itself.

"You interested in the living truth?" I ask.

"Don't catch your meaning precisely," he says, cuts his eyes at me, and snags a willow branch. He's lost his timing.

" 'The wages of sin is death,' " I say.

"The Good Book tells it all," he says, and I watch a drop of sweat slide from his hair line down along his temple and cheek to hang off his chin. He wipes a palm under it.

"We in agreement," I say.

"Every man should try to live by the Word," he says.

"And die by it," I say.

He reels in, sets the rod aside quick, and glances at me but won't hold my eye. He begins paddling toward Miller's Bridge.

"Look here, Matthew, I get the feeling you telling me

something," he says. His face has become sweat shiny, and his brow catches a spot of glow from a lightning bug. He swats at it.

"No I have done telling," I say. What I've been doing is watching the river broaden out to where it's now three to four feet deep.

"You may have gotten the wrong idea about certain things," he says.

"What things?" I ask.

"People talking and telling all kinds of tales when they don't know all the facts," he says. "I'd like for you and me to be friends. Do some fishing together."

"Sounds good to me," I say and hold out my hand. When he smiles, leans toward me, and shakes it, I yank him hard, club him with my left fist, and haul him beside me from the boat. 'Fore he can holler, I shove him under. He thrashes, but he's not much man. Whatever does Jessie see in him?

"Won't take long," I tell bubbles of his silent screaming face. Like drowning a cat.

It's full night, and the boat drifts downriver. I pull Philip ashore, heave him over my shoulder, and dump him. I hike through the pine woods edging the paved secondary to my truck. I drive back, load Philip into the bed, and cover him with shovel loads of barn droppings.

I circle Red Oak in case big eyes is looking out windows. In the low ground I left my John Deere with the front-end ditcher attached. I dig the hole, refill it, and draw the harrow's teeth across the ground to pattern it with the rest of the field already prepared for sowing a new crop of winter wheat. Moon glimmer covers the land.

Philip's johnboat is found half sunk against the river's south bank near Clarksville. They drag for the body. I watch Jessie's face as she hears the news from the radio. Her expression don't change, but she joins hands at her waist and tightens them so hard the fingers whiten.

We have rains, causing our wheat to sprout. The field takes on a sheen. Searchers stop looking for Philip. Some believe fish has nibbled him away or he got cut up in turbine blades of Virginia Power's Hidden River dam. At the school a new principal's in charge.

The day before Thanksgiving I shoot a twelve-pound gobbler in a gang ranging for weed seeds among chopped stalks of the fallow cornfield. I pluck and gut the bird, which Jessie roasts for our dinner the next day after church services.

While she's finishing up in the kitchen, I call her to come stand on our porch. It's a cool sunny afternoon, and I have her look out over the wheat, which gleams like a calm green sea all the way to cedars bounding our property.

"Let us give the good Lord thanks for an abundant crop," I tell her.

As I pray she bows her head, and her fingers struggle beneath the white dish towel draped over them.

ABOUT THE AUTHOR

A master storyteller, award-winning William Hoffman is the author of three previous short-story collections and eleven novels, most recently the acclaimed *Tidewater Blood*. His work has appeared in numerous magazines and anthologies.